THE UNDERACHIEVER

A (n anti) Novel

Pablo Saborío

SPUYTEN DUYVIL
New York City

ISBN 978-1-963908-46-6

First Edition: October 2024

Cover image: Pablo Saborío

Spuyten Duyvil
223 Bedford Ave.
PMB #725
Brooklyn, NY 11211
https://spuytenduyvil.net/

Library of Congress Control Number: 2024947711

You will never leave anything that remotely resembles a footprint, much less a mark, in the rich soil of Western literature.

—The Editor

I lack talent. Take this sentence, it's dying. Much of what I write sinks to the floorboards. Quite mad to consider that I've published three novels. Two. The third one never got out of the printing house. How I have done it surpasses explanation. Never have I told a good story, no genius plot to dazzle my readers. All but a jumble of impressions, often disjointed reflections that nobody would care to unravel. My style appeals to no one. I started by imitating my greats—Pynchon, Cortázar, Nabokov—but I did not even reach the heights of their toenails. So, I turned to my lesser greats: Camus, Orwell, Hemingway, and a bunch of US-Americans[1]. I wrote my first two books fighting the liberality of my graphomania by imitating writers with a simple prose line, though I was mediocre at that too. Lyrical, convoluted, and often incomprehensible sentences belie my determination to keep my prose lucid. I was stunned when *the* editor at Nord Dam, a leading avantgarde publishing house, accepted my first manuscript. Knowing him beforehand undoubtedly played a role—as is the incestuous way of the literary world—but he could have easily dismissed my first, feeble efforts to become a published novelist from the outset.

The first novel, a novella if you ask me, described a room. A person, of undefined gender (though any versed reader could detect the awkwardness of a penis-bearing creature), studies

____

1 I don't call them Americans because America is an entire continent. Imagine a German proclaiming their national identity as European, to the exclusion of every other European. Here in Europe, we speak *Hochdeutsch*. We Europeans have faith in our *Bundestag*. Europe is the land of speed. Absurd!

a room the day before he is going to die. The main character does not know he is about to die. The reader does, however, so I attempted to infuse every detail with absolute meaning since it was the last time this person would ever encounter all those things in themselves, whatever they were. My debut bestseller was, after failing to come up with a more alluring title, titled: *The Room*. It is a tedious read; few make it halfway though it is only ninety pages. Immediately after its release, however, two critics created a big buzz in a leading newspaper and in a small, but influential literary journal. I was hailed as a pioneer in the nascent school of Detailism. The concept caught on and the first edition—a measly 2,000 copies—sold out. Still, I would bet less than ten people finished the book. Nonetheless, there I found myself, riding the wave of Detailism, a style that thrives by dismantling the grand narratives the "tyrannical" past has enforced upon us.

When you are spearheading a literary movement, you should not shift gears more rapidly than the market can keep pace with. My second novel, also a novella in my eyes, is called *Things;* a short, unimaginative remake of that contrarian impulse to rescue literature from its "supercilious" heights. I just kept writing about things as they looked, felt, or behaved; while neglecting narrative in a sort of Husserlian kaleidoscope of impressions, with total disregard to any underlying logic that might explain why things emerge and fade in consciousness as they do. If I can persuade readers to wade through this kind of garrulous poetic labyrinth, the prospect of a fourth book remains.

The third one, which was denied entry into the world, carries this title: *The Life of Objects*. Of course, it's not life as we comprehend it. It's a poetic narration of life from the perspective of things, in non-linear fashion, so commonplace objects may appear for a brief moment in the book, before the reader is transported to another faraway location, where similar but unrecognizable objects are presented. Geography is lost, purpose is nullified, objects are portrayed as they exist in-themselves (as if they could exist elsewise) then lost from view without notice, as if below the world's surface were a giant current of nothingness that creeps in and out of the horizon of perception to reveal things that are and certainly will be nothing. This last sentence exemplifies my incorrigible style: orotund, barely understandable prattle.

Narratives are inescapable, though. Take my first book. I had to place the descriptions of the room within the setting of a person dying in twenty-four hours. A storyline is implied, a barge to ferry words across the river of time. Always water. Can't keep it out of my writing. Take the first sentence of *The Room*: "The surface of the bed developed naturally into a sea of ripples." What a pitiful display of the mundane: a sea of ripples. When had I last even looked at the sea? Why couldn't I have conceived a richer image? Like wind-brushed dunes. Or the corrugated skin of an elephant. That's why I never dwell too long on an image. Subsequent attempts still leave a flavor of mediocrity in my mouth. Language can hardly transcend the world it emerges from. Woodlice will only bear woodlice. Language is the offspring of the world. But hold on a minute, could the opposite be true? Can the world be the offspring of language? The world as we know it, full of objects and relationships, which are defined semantically in the mind before they can be apprehended as such, can, after all, only arise once the underlying structure of language has solidified in the brain. It seems like hair-splitting—a classic example of armchair philosophizing. Often it is hunger that interrupts my reflections. Won't ever amount to the title of philosopher, not with this appetite anyway. Briskly buttering bread for bedtime bite. Ah, an alliteration!

Clearly, I have yet to make much progress. That's why I keep chaining myself—factually—to this desk every midnight for three hours. A sadistic act that yields scant Parnassian harvests. The harder I try, the more irrelevant all this seems. Truth be told, I never got the point of the writing game. To win the game you must follow the rules cleverly, breaking them strategically, only to reach higher up the board while pretending you've been playing it straight all along. I've given a lot of thought to the game's objective. Validation, recognition, fame, success. Success is an emergent property of failure. That is, failure is the bedrock of existence. The awareness that you will ultimately fail drives you to fulfill bigger ambitions, even as you keep failing. You must fail repeatedly, to the point where you feel you can never get up again. Time, like a soft invisible balm, soothes your hurts. Memory forgets to remember. And you try again. Not necessarily learning from your mistakes as much as not caring if you fail again or how you plan to win. A callous heart, insensitive to the blows of fate, begins to conquer the world. The only catch is that you no longer sincerely enjoy your achievements when they arrive. I was a stone-faced Stoic at my first book launch. I yawn reading the good reviews of my books. I achieved a modicum of success, but my hunger for more eclipses any sense of satisfaction. When I finished the third novel, I barely had any desire to write. Or read. Life's faint spark receded further into the emptiness. I stopped attending the intense psychedelic parties my artists friends were throwing. I gave up any idea of joining a circling session to tap into the unknown powers of the unconscious. I ceased traveling, meeting people, listening to mind-expanding podcasts. I found some joy in watching football, a weak delight when looking at passersby's faces full of young optimism. But am I playing the game anymore? Not in the least. The image of ash keeps coming to my mind. The ash of paper. The cinder of fame. The smokescreen of success, hiding an aberrant appetite that the world can never satisfy.

When my friend died, I felt something. It was the first tentacle stemming as a tendril from death's amorphous body. Death became a living thing, breathing behind my back. I became a Buddhist without understanding a single sutra or meditating a proper hour. My attention shifted from the outer to the inner. Watching each little sensation appear and vanish within seconds. There was only impermanence, I would think—and in those early days, I would get drunk, because what did it matter. Those were lively days full of purpose as I discovered the power of nihilism. I could write my doggerel with unbounded pride— "To work and create for nothing" —and laugh, as definitive as a Biblical commandment, but it came from Camus's monumental *Myth*[2]. The absurdity of this finite adventure is

____

2 If I were to be imprisoned in a cellar by a fascist government and had the option to take only one book, it would be this one. Schopenhauer's 'Essays

plain and transparent for all to see. My dictum was clear: I will disappear *ergo* I must write. Life was obvious; the future spewed its futility like a volcano about to bleach my horizons with a coat of white ash. Drink, write, and feel above the masses because you're staring Death straight in the eye.

Twenty years ago, I was on top of the world as I hung over— pun intended—an unfathomable abyss. Today the abyss has shrunk to the size of a pothole. Whether I notice the world's insignificance or not, what consequence does that have? I have broken through to a new paradigm: meta-nihilism. My friend would have never reached this standstill, he was the epitome of *carpe diem*. A far superior nihilist than I, while never once giving a single thought to life's impermanence. He could drink deeper into the night, seduce bodies *ad libitum*, wake up without complaint though he puked into midafternoon every Saturday and Sunday. Women, men, children came to him to absorb his guileless zest for living in the moment. Like nothing mattered: money, girls, prestige. He would pay for everybody's drinks until he reached a euphoria impossible to subdue. Then the show began. A dark flaming intellect scorched the soft edges of meaning. The "Midnight Sun from Iceland" —a terrible long-winded nickname that stuck for years—had reached the tropics.

His death was so poetic, beyond anything I could possibly compose. We were traveling in Nicaragua, drinking day and

and Aphorisms' would be a close second. If lost in the woods, I might opt for something short along the lines of Kerouac's 'Dharma Bums' or even 'Franny and Zooey' from that real-life Bartleby. In the event of being adrift at sea on a makeshift raft, 'Meditations' by Marcus Aurelius would do me well. If I end up in a madhouse, I'd only read Clarice Lispector. If homeless, wandering barefoot in a city; I'd carry anything by Cortázar with me.

night, meeting girls, climbing up volcanoes, listening to Radiohead, discussing Vallejo and Parra, playing cards and guitars, dancing merengue, eating rice and beans as our only sustenance. We met a Spanish girl, Eva, with whom we both fell desperately in love after just a few hours in San Juan del Sur. A wild girl, with exquisite tattoos, breathing in more *mota* than air, curvaceous as a spiral of wind on sand. We paid an islander for a round boat trip and walked the island's coast, waiting to be picked up before nightfall. My friend and I enjoyed our typical case of beers each as we explored the coastline, while Eva studied the fish, shells, and sea urchins. My friend was on to fate, how he believed there was no free will, that everything was destined to happen exactly as it did. He ventured further out into the sea, atop spiky rocks whose tips rose above the surface of the water like the heads of ancient titans queuing toward the horizon, while I followed him hesitantly. He had reached his euphoric state and was talking about the Tao of water (Watts), messages in the wind (Dylan/Shamanism), the superfluous complexity of consciousness (Cioran) and the cryptic endings of Kafka's novels. Just when, from the furthest rock out in the sea, he began reciting by heart the last lines of *The Castle*, he was swallowed and never seen again; consumed by the sea, by the world's appetite, by the dark unknown that hungers beneath the earth we know.

I lost touch with Eva even though we fell asleep that night in mid-act, my penis limp like a sea cucumber inside the drying shell of her vulva. We could not finish after we had just seen the biggest end of all. I continued traveling further north, increasingly disbelieving each word I read, dismantling any ideology that could have sent me to the frontlines of activism, reveling in knowing that pain and silence will gorge the feast of lived experience.

Naturally, for any recollection to be true, I need to remember accurately, retain some fidelity with the mode the events unfolded in—maintain, through memory's sobering refraction, the mood we were in, the conversations we had, the meaning of what happened. I'm not sure this last part, especially, can ever be retrieved or properly expounded. Each time I replay the sequence of his death, something is changed, a bit is omitted, a new detail emerges, not to mention the bodily effects that thinking of the past can trigger. An anachronistic hard-on may bring me back years before that night at the beach, to women who extracted volumes of fears I had no idea waited deep inside me; or spring me forward to a much later date in Europe, when, as I was ejaculating inside a woman, I visualized the inertia of that fall into the lukewarm Pacific seawater as identical to the force of my semen against the walls of her uterus. That thrust clustered my sperm around an ovule and brought from uterine darkness the light of a child I would call my own, while my friend, the antipodal Midnight Sun, joyous in the throes of uncertainty, optimistic while lost in the fog of thought, descended from this world of light into the darkest of the dark.

> *you are a man of no talent, an abstract blob who writes poetic riddles, linguistic mirages that can be taken for anything by a readership that today can be as easily swayed as a weathervane.*

It's 2:58AM, and shortly, I'll be released from my self-imposed shackles. Nothing of true literary value in these pages. A whimsical ledger of thoughts as they skim across the paper-thin membrane of my intellect. This is not writing. This is not art. It is a form of wrestling, grappling with time, simulating a grand struggle with language inside the irreducibly eternal ring of silence. I'm exhausted, waiting for the final blow to knock me to the ground, an impact so definitive it will obliterate my last vestige of urgency to impose meaning onto the messy Pollock of reality. What's that? More convoluted, overwrought images. But it is not only my inability to master the craft of prose writing that exasperates me. I cringe every time I observe how the absurdity of language disfigures reality.

Language is concealment. It hides *The Great Enigma*. What is *The Great Enigma*? It is the inscrutable *Mystery* at the bottom of all things, the *Riddle* that governs the universe. It is like a centrifugal force that keeps us running in circles, inventing cures, building higher, traveling faster, an impetus that will eventually drive us to develop an AI-controlled planet. Language can never apprehend *that* ontological desire coursing below the skin of events, that primordial impulse behind the thrust of evolution, the raw force that gives birth to both beauty and havoc, light and darkness, the Ying-Yang's *élan vital* so intrinsic to nature, our nature, our urge to keep wading through the morass of

No need to complete what cannot be finished. That's why I ought to keep things simple. Find a clean passage through the thickness of my obscurantism. To cease systematically squandering the strength of logic, blunting the once incisive blade of thought. I am bound to keep writing, it is 3:07AM and will not stop until I have the kernel of a new story: The lamp is almost invisible; we only see the illuminated objects around it. The pack of cards rests on the desk. The dust of decades has now become a new skin around the widgets of the Canon A-1 camera that sleeps below the lamp.

Maybe the hope is that if I bore myself to death this tautology of imbecility might cease.

Let's have another go. The lamp stoops in a melancholy posture, as do I. We both stare at the dust as it settles over the 50-year-old camera. Analogue past, sidelined by a digital future. Oh my. I should have stuck with erotica. I was writing that for some time and even got serialized under the pseudonym Don Humbert H. in the local progressive newspaper. The story was titled "The Breasts of Wrath." Hardly a winning title, it nonetheless had its fair share of readers. I tried to reach the level of high-brow erotica. Fortunately, the editors requested that I keep the language as simple as possible—quotidian babble with few philosophical asides—such that the aroused reader could easily follow the mischief of my horny characters. Advice I took gladly so as not to completely embarrass myself with my absolute lack of literary prowess.

The camera's lid has been lost for years. The lens is pointed toward a deck of cards that is yellowing around the edges. The motes of dust gravitate around the lamp's light; when he stares without blinking, he feels like he is watching trillions of suns in their two-hundred-million-year treks around the core of a distant galaxy. He keeps the passport next to the cards. Ready to flee at a moment's notice. His sense of imminent danger has escalated dramatically over the past weeks. Doom is around the corner. The radical revelation, known to earlier civilizations as the *apocalypse*, was about to materialize, spill over, like a wave of such potent change—we could only label it as a creative disaster. But he knew it would do more than kickstart a new promising beginning. The prophets of the ultra-modern, who claimed the earlier modalities of life would be changed forever for the better through a new social contract forged by enlightened humans, were delusional. He alone could understand the physics of the coming revolution. The latest chapter in humanity's struggle would unfold as irrevocably as a trickle feeds a stream, a stream turns into river, river becomes a torrent, torrent expands into an irrepressible force that will burst the dam of our self-sustaining paradigms. The prophets call it the waters of wisdom washing over the forsaken land. The prophets could not foresee that, as he did, the flood would leave us in the mud of our ignorance. Havoc will ensue, the famished, unawakened folk will unite to fight the radical policies of the wise leaders. In short, the few awakened ones will be buried by their blind contemporaries. He knew it as certain as a semantic tableau and was therefore preemptively ready to flee the struggle before it began, to hide away from the renaissance of the future's culture, the reform of our civilization that would ultimately end in bloodshed and misery—as all revolutions in the past had ended.

Midnight again. A new beginning. When I started writing I decided to do it on my own. The pride of youth. In hindsight, I've handicapped myself by not getting enough critical feedback, hindering my writing from evolving beyond the echo chamber of my own mind. Now that I'm in my mid-forties, I've considered starting from scratch. Join a creative writing class, maybe even take a bachelor's degree in world literature. I'll fake ignorance and pretend to be a total beginner. Allow a teacher to purify the eschatological tendencies of my prose. I need classmates that will thwart my thoughts from blinding themselves in the skies of abstraction, I want the weight of criticism to stop these flights into abstruse illegibility. I could even use the mentorship of a classicist so they can help me recast ancient myths into novel poetic arrangements (by drawing me nearer to the sun's blazing truth, thawing the icy grip of my ego, so that my unfettered fingers can channel the rivers of verse into a singular, horizon-spanning masterpiece). Basically, I need to come clean, naked as an amateur dreamer that one day wants to write the next *Gatsby* or a 21st century *Lolita*. A dream that will be quickly squashed when they read my puny attempts at elevating the English language—a borrowed language—to the levels of High Literature.

Poetry could have been a better route. I wrote a few poems back in the day. They showed a bit more promise. I walk two steps

      into the future. The scurrying mouse is a fiction.
This cloud tucked in
    the sky
    exactly like the idea
of death
when it is folded neatly   inside your right pocket.

Death has always been in my mind. Even before my friend died. Suicidal tendencies tainted most of my teenage years. I can't recall when the void first became palpable but one day it was there, beneath my skin, on the surface of my eyes, on my father's moustache, in my mother's melancholy, at the edge of my school desk, beneath the bed, in the substance of every night's dream. Death diluted the world's title of true existence. There was no joy left. The spectacle of life became a sort of sorry excuse to postpone the extinction of meaning. To achieve honors at school, exceed in sports, conquer the most hearts of the opposite or same sex, to learn how to play guitar; every goal had lost its gravity. I stopped smiling, not caring what others would say. Shaved my head and my right eyebrow.

Stopped paying attention in class. I programmed myself to fail. Locked myself in a room that I kept as dark as the void I had discovered.

What's your plan for college would return a *Does it matter, when we're all eventually demoted to the grave?*

What is your dream job would be dismissed with *What will it matter in 30 million years?*

But it was not as bleak as it may sound. It ultimately depends on the story I fashion around my memories of the past. There were joys in those youthful days. Watching Wrestle-Mania while secretly drinking a six-pack in my room. Conceiving cheating techniques for school exams with my friends over the phone. Throwing rocks as streetlights. Going to those first unisex parties while trying to dance with two legs as stiff as stilts and a hip as rusty as a Cuban Volkswagen. But after each experience there was this lingering sense of emptiness, that nothing had been achieved, nothing had come close to filling the bottomless abyss at the center of life. There was only one solution, one viable escape to this endless predicament: suicide. I set a date and was going to kill myself by the age of nineteen. I was around sixteen years old when I made this resolution. In the three years I had left, I felt I had nothing to fight for, the end was in view. I threw myself drunk into barbwire. I masturbated relentlessly. I began to curse humanity in the first emails I sent out to friends and acquaintances. I was ready to burn it all, with a rage as wide as the dumb silence that enveloped me. Then I turned nineteen, I forgot about my resolution. I missed my chance to redeem myself as an achiever, a go-getter. There was no alternative other than to become a ~~miserable~~ writer.

When I became of age, an intellectual itch began to nag me. What is this temporary illusion all about? I became obsessed with trying to understand everything. Cognitive dissonance at its best. Later on, I would realize that we can never transcend our self-deception, but back in those early days, I was trying to reach the kernel of existence. Looking for the key to the configuration of society, science, evolution, religion, consciousness, you name it. Silly theatrics, if you ask me; like accruing all the money in the world only to light it up in one momentary blaze. Decipher the *Mystery* so your knowledge can dissolve when your heart stops beating. The contradiction was evident, but I kept at it. It took me many years to stumble upon *the* insuperable fallacy. The problem, in a nutshell, is that you can't solve an illusion by using the language that resides in that illusory reality. It's like doing calculus in a dream. How was I going to break through the veil of the mortal fog by using the spirals of misty logic to clear the blur?

Now this puny selection of anecdotes and reflections reveals more of who I am today rather than who I was back then. I could equally dwell on more uplifting episodes of my life, equally formative as the so-called suicidal years. My years backpacking on a shoestring. My time as an exchange student in the US (*of* America). The night at a beach in the south of Spain that I spent telling (the worst) jokes all night, so terrible that people couldn't get enough of them. I could build on a story that could inspire people. But no, I keep recalling the pathos in my life. This penchant to reveal the somber in me is more indicative of an insecure person looking for empathy; well, not empathy—let me say it flat out, I crave validation. I feel insufficient. Whatever potential I might have, has been wasted by careless procrastination. It's only 1:48AM, and the pink fur of this BDSM collar is already making my neck itch. I should have built in an override setting so I could unlock myself from my desk when necessary. I need to keep writing to lose track of time.

Time plays the dirtiest tricks. Perhaps one day there will be a mental shift in me, and I will no longer aspire to become a respectable writer. I'll go into permaculture or forest preservation. I could find unalloyed happiness running a small bed and breakfast close to the sea. I'll limit my reading to the daily newspaper and the sports section of the *Guardian*. Life could be simple and sweet, a stroll along the beach, caressing smooth pebbles in my hands while I gaze into the boundless arc of the horizon.

I've spent a good deal of time mentally preparing for that ghastly denouement—I harden the skin of my expectations so when the bullet of regret hits me straight in the chest, there'll be a little less to kill. Who am I fooling? I'll be worth less than nothing if I ever decide to quit writing. I'd rather be an impotent writer in old age than a person who lives contentedly in the now of his last years.

There are three families, deeply linked to the movement of primordial Earth. Over millions of years, they have grown to dizzying heights that have left us as snails in the shadow of their monstrosity. Columns tall as the Hyperion tree in linear formation like some remote cathedral erected by the bubbling murmur of underground heat. Swirls caught in the prism of an alien rainbow, preserving in each layer the patience of colossal* time. From these prototypical Abraham-Isaac-Jacob of the rocks, the architecture of our planet, through igneous, sedimentary, and metamorphic transformations, has been set for the late drama of the last ape.

An epic of gargantuan proportions, beginning with the formation of the earth, all the way to the self-destruction of the human race, that'd be the climax of my (literary) desires. That is, whenever I get an inclination to play the game again. It will also be the greatest disappointment, having surpassed the toughest challenge, leaving the mind exempt from the need for a higher objective. Imagine having finished *Gravity's Rainbow*. What's next? You might as well start life over. Remove yourself from society to polish amber stones in a tiny hut by the Baltic Sea or move to the Faroe Islands to hunt for whale.

Lately I get strange sensations in the middle of the night after I finish my trussed writing sessions. My insides feel as if they are constantly shifting. I can almost sense each organ slowly slithering into a new location. The heart moves into the base of the stomach, the stomach pushes the liver into the right lung. The lungs squeeze out all the air to contract into the position of the kidneys. While I experience this—obviously, a psychosomatic hallucination—I close my eyes and detect countless luminous figures swirling behind my eyelids. I must lie down on my desk and take long deep breaths. After ten minutes or so, the thing passes. I believe it is my nervous system about to collapse. Or my brain deteriorating to a degree it can no longer receive accurate impressions from the body. I've made it this far with Damocles' piercing blade above my thoughts. Any day, when I least expect it, the curtain will drop.

How deranged will I be when it's time for time to cease? I can foresee all sorts of bizarre diseases crippling my body. And yet, what frightens me the most are those unpredictable detours from the realm of sanity. The mind seems like an incredibly fragile container. A few hours of intense torture, two days without sleep, a microgram of some powerful psychedelic and its pretty structure comes hurtling down. The walls of memory are brittle. The amygdala can flare up and overwhelm us with cataclysmic emotions. Even the sensation of the "I" wobbles like a soap bubble under the stress of the tiniest friction. I've spent more hours than I could count studying the "I". At first, I thought that if I could disprove its actuality, then whatever element of consciousness remains would be freed from the absurdity of living and dying. I looked deeply to find the space the "I" occupies. Like the Scot, I found a jumble of impressions and sensations, coming in and out of awareness, under their own rule and law. Any aspect of this deep-rooted "I" could only be confirmed within the field of experience. To know the "I", there must be a subjective impression. An awareness of something: an itch on the leg – my leg. A thought of worry – my worry. Irrepressible fear – my fear. Whatever quality this "I" may have, must first be experienced in awareness. But guess what, I could never actually find the "I" behind the experiences. It was implied to be there, the thinker of the thoughts, the feeler of feelings, the *primum movens* of actions. A lovely assumption, except we never get to see that nucleus behind every idea, emotion, or behavior. It was at this stage that I clearly began to realize we're under the spell of a very cunning illusion. The illusion of the self. A thought that frightens me because I believe it could trigger a precocious senility. I can foresee it: my perception bleeding out into the external world, memories evaporating in the speed of that hemorrhage, the mind emptying itself of all its contents, leaving only a diaphanous picture of NOW, where no thing can be fully grasped; all the maps of reality I've worked hard to build will be as good as trails charted on seaside sand a fortnight ago.

Recycling ideas as always. How much of that dread is based on actual lived truth? I read a couple books about mysticism, heard a few talks by Alan Watts (a hero of the Midnight Sun), maybe read some Krishnamurti, perhaps got get a glimpse of some non-personal level of reality when I took a heroic dose of MDMA and shrooms too many years ago to accurately remember the experience. Ideas seem to float in my head, myriad lenses that zoom in and out on different levels of reality, I speak firsthand of subjects I've only read about, thoughts horde the mind like a swarm of cicadas, but they are too scattered and disfigured to ever construct a solid philosophical system. In my mid-twenties I proudly proclaimed myself a dilettante, happy to write these kinds of nonsensical philosophical vignettes; today, twenty years later, I read the above paragraph and I give myself the title of pseudo-intellectual. Everything I write rings empty to me. In fact, I'm starving.

Naan bread smothered in Nutella and peanut butter. I should cut down on so much bread, it's making me bloated. Constantly gaining weight, I can't resist inspecting every new little nook fat keeps inventing as its new habitat. There's no telling how my face will end up looking in the next twenty years. It will probably resemble an elephant seal; I'll be this despicable old timer that I must come to accept as myself, just because that's the face I'll meet in the mirror. Whatever shape I assume will be taken to be me if I am trapped inside it. Makes me wonder if we are not something completely alien to human life, a cosmic point of condensed hyperdimensional vision, an iota of awareness hiding from its infinite imaginative power in order to embody an imperfect avatar, a puppet that allows it to get delightfully lost in the fear and delights of a mortal life. Seriously? Did I just write that hysterical metaphysics? I should substitute bread with rice cakes.

Every now and then I get into the habit of rereading those trite stacks of paper I've written in the past. I was such a dreamer at the start. I would conceive images as crude as the sappy lyrics of a 19th century Romantic. As always, I've been pulled by contradictory impulses. At that time, I intended to write prose that could be universally admired, yet I wanted to avoid falling into the derisory tricks of a best-selling author. I wanted to be respected by academia yet adored by the masses. I'm not embarrassed to admit such puerile desire. Fame is an irresistible charm for a young mind.

The Anatomy of a Life

… but still a faint light glared under the menace of dark annihilation, his memory, though severely battered by time, retained the core of his experiences and as the last ticking second of the clock of his life came closer, his passion was poured out through the tip of his pen. The candle on his desk flickered to and fro, resisting its own death when a strong breeze came gushing down through the chimney. The light of his memory similarly faced extinction, as it battled with the ailments of old age.

Have I evolved as a writer? Clearly not. It's still the same melodramatic BS my mind keeps spewing out to this day and age, I had that thought about ten years ago when I first revisited my short story from which I took this excerpt. There is no doubt I had that thought because I have a dated note next to it stating: "*Have I evolved as a writer? Clearly not. It's still the same melodramatic BS my mind keeps spewing out to this day and age.*" The note has faded, but I can almost remember writing each condemning letter. I was thinking just now, if I were to ask the question again: have I made progress with my literary skills? Did I transform myself into a different kind of writer through my involuntary ventures into Detailism? Could I ever write another novel that can be published, or will I be destined to write this puzzling outpour of pure balderdash? I feel a thick lump of silence stuck in my throat. A sensation I will keep having every time I take out and reread *The Anatomy of a Life*, I think.

That's plagiarism. Always trying to imitate rather than create *ex nihilo*. Anybody can easily tell that's a terrible parody of Thomas Bernhard. But others also took from him. When I first read Sebald, I knew this guy had devoured Bernhard. A style that is unmistakable. I sigh, I am sighing right now, because I'm such a melodramatic thespian. Wishing my sentences could be long, unending fractals extending deeper into the story until you lose sight of your point of departure and have no clue where the text is leading you. I will confess; I envy Bernhard's ability to write a book without taking a single breath.

At some point, out of plain frustration, I started to break free from the romanticism of the aspiring writer who wants to win the hearts of humankind. I started looking for works that are demanding, critical and elusive. In short, I discovered the freedom and playfulness of postmodern literature. Works that are probably only read by other writers, to learn, copy or plagiarize from the newly emergent styles. Only one out of one hundred postmodern writers are a joy to read. The rest are... well, like me.

PREFACE

I will not pretend to disclose in this essay anything that can be deemed original. My discourse is simply a clarification of aspects already present everywhere, processes constantly in action and easily recognizable by any human that takes a moment to reflect on these things. Thus, my philosophy is nothing we can call a discovery, or even the creation of an unorthodox perspective. What I attempt in the following pages is to give clear definition to the content of our experience. I will take the liberty to appropriate the vernacular and add nuances to its ordinary meaning. Whenever I formulate a fuller meaning for a common word, I will continue to capitalize the word. For example, my study of the idea of property leads me to question the functioning of consciousness vis-a-vis experience. After I introduce the problem and my prospective solution, the word Property will appear as that now global concept that interacts in the new established context, connected to novel and often conflicting concepts and fields not ordinarily associated with its normal signification, but, if studied carefully, will be shown to be nonetheless functional and verifiable at all times.

EXCERPT FROM THE INTRODUCTION

The present is ownerless. It does not belong to any entity, ego or being. This Present is the purest form of existence, the quality, medium and category of anything that ever exists. The Form of the Present cannot be apprehended by what we call the mind. The mind is only an aspect of the Present, a modulation of the Form the Present achieves through complicated methods to provide us (imagined entities) with the conception or concept of Mind. The Present is ownerless, but this does not imply it is boundless or infinite in every manifestation. It has a particular flavor, recurrent Forms within the purity of its essential FORM. Only the **judgment** that it belongs to a body, a life, a person, constitutes its being possessed by that imagined entity. The movement of the Present is indeed the only Entity that delves into its own Essence to experience an individualization of Form in its Mind. With this in mind, we can begin grasping the significance of knowledge. Knowledge is the Form of the Present detained or sustained momentarily for the Forms of the Mind to apprehend it. Knowledge reduces itself to a solipsism of extreme kind. It is Essence looking into Pure Form of Mind while the Present acts as Entity confronted by the Experience of movement in Forms. Thus, Knowledge behaves like the mythological snake that endlessly eats its own tail. To establish the rules of Knowledge within the framework of undifferentiated Pure FORM, the Present solidifies certain Aspects (recurrent Forms) of its Movement to establish the basis of Class. Classification of Forms is the *a priori* condition for Philosophical Knowledge to exist as a study of Essence. How then can the illusion of the Ego exist as a solitary unit of Solidity within the Flux of Essence? There is no answer to this question, and I will endeavor to meticulously and systematically prove this in this book with my definition of the Present.

I don't think I ever finished that story. It was meant to be about a book within a book. An esoteric philosopher reflecting about his thoughts while showing us—the readers—excerpts of his work. The life of this philosopher was afflicted by constant trials. He smoked three packs of cigarettes a day. Was addicted to bacon and masturbation. Would have an obsessive compulsion to finish reading a book a day. Earned a living by scamming people online and lived in constant fear that the police would come knocking at his smoked-filled room.

It was at midnight some years back, I was thinking a moment ago, when I first realized I needed to radically change my style. Strip my writing of its meandering verbosity, that incorrigible baroque impulse to adorn every tip of language. So, I started experimenting and was satisfied as well as relieved with the results but could never get beyond a paragraph or two.

There is a window. Inside it a color. Orange. Nothing but that color within the frame. An eerie orange, between tangerine and saffron. I walk toward the window. Peer into that totality of color. There is depth. Looking closely, I see another room. Chairs, tables, glasses, everything orange, just a slightly darker shade. There is time within the frame of the window. Objects are moving. Changes take place. As if the room were inhabited by ghosts. Fiery figures the color of carrots. A story is taking place. I lean in and hear the frame vibrate. A story emerges, it speaks: every color is a desire. Within each desire, there are fragments of smaller cravings. Each little appetite gets a border, a shape as a vessel to move in the picture. We identify the aspects of desire as objects, everyday things. They resemble symbols. Living metaphors. You are witnessing a tiny arena, like peering into a cell's nucleus. The orchestra of life. The chair is tucked under the table. The glass is taken to the cupboard. The cushion receives an indentation. A book is opened. Page 97. Inside the book, other colors. Lilac. Violet. Periwinkle. The letters inside the book are also moving, ghost-like signifiers embodying meaning through spatial interactions. The word 'ROOM' stretches itself to encompass the word 'MOUSE'. The word 'ANIMAL' merges with the word 'BREATHING'. The word 'LIGHT' makes the word 'WALL' ripple in its wake. The word 'AWAKENS' comes closer as the word 'BODY' suddenly, almost magically, emerges. The word 'WOMAN' strides through the emptiness of the word 'ROOM'. The word 'SHRIEK' burgeons as billows of smoke within the word 'AIR'. The word 'MOUSE' recedes into the infinite horizon we read as 'MOUSE

HOLE'. I peer closer into the tiny abyss. I discover another color...

Eventually I was able to write two book-length texts, which were acts of imitation and restriction rather than pure imaginative creation. The results, *The Room* and *Things*, should have been nothing but steppingstones, the stuff of juvenilia, leading to a cogent, composed, poetically refined style of prose that I could uniquely call mine. *The Life of Objects* was a retrogression if anything, and all this new text is nothing short of a farce.

Let me return to meta-nihilism. I've stared at the abyss. Menacing, unfathomable desiccator of all meaning. Pay attention to that. We qualify the abyss as something intimidating, we project into it the emptiness of purpose; we label it as terrifying. But what if you just stare at it, not even knowing it is an abyss? Not interpreting it as an empty expanse. A dumb stare. Looking not with indifference but plain ignorance. Not even asking for the meaning of meaninglessness. The abyss dwindles. It is a puddle you step over. A dry leaf carried by the wind. A hiccup that momentarily interrupts your train of thought. That's it. We stopped being reactive to nothingness. So, what if nothing really matters? Don't resist, don't favor. Don't wish for things to be different. Don't try to blow up the world, because ultimately it will fail. Don't measure how deep the absurdity is. Don't trust your certainty that there is nothing real. Don't assume you understand the width of existence's futility. I gaze into the abyss, and the abyss shrinks into ice cream. I'm hungry.

There are two parallel branches in my life that are leading into dead ends. The first, literally. My attempts at literature are getting nowhere. The second branch, which I would rather call a trunk, is my body. It is exponentially gaining volume. Last month I weighed 113 kgs. I might have gained 5 kgs since. My appetite is growing in exact relation to my new erratic writings. For every ten pages I write, I gain a kilo. I shall be a bulbous dead whale within a year.

Lily fucks a stream. Naked and horny under a full moon, she coils her legs around a tree. The galaxy has a desire that travels like electricity through its roots. Her vulva's lips warmly embracing the rough chunks of bark exuding from the trunk. She howls before jumping into the water. Here the force of the stream thickens as an invisible phallus that penetrates her. Lily is in tears. Her fluids unite with the night-blue waters. The river moans in delight as Lily comes, over and over, against the rocks and pebbles that course down toward the now-kindling horizon. Her skin becomes bubbles, small domes of pleasure reflecting the entire empire of air. She drinks in the foam with insatiable thirst; love is a transmutation of world into human, woman into time. The morning light concentrates on her retina. A new world emerges ready to be fucked.

I've always wanted to write a cosmic erotica, an animalistic journey into the procreation of a novel universe. To somehow escape the narrow confines of reason and rekindle mythological thinking. To stretch the credibility of language to the point where you are lost in the bliss of pure image. Condensation of sensation inside the concave spoon of metaphor. To place a mouthful of absolute imagination into the terrifying gape of the mind, to sever reality from chronology, to leave the body as the abandoned husk of the past, so we can finally enter the translucent intensity of a world vibrating in mute timelessness.

Let's try that again. I want to create a new genre of erotica by inducing an animalistic mindset through the alchemy of mythical thinking. In this work, humans are active participants in the reproduction of a new universe. I want to generate a cosmic orgasm by leaving the straitjacket of reason behind. To watch language drop the husk of logic and move into the pure ecstasy of an unmeasurable image. I crave to see all sensation gather densely inside the tightest metaphor. To drink this honey for the mind to lose all reference as to what is real: reality must become feral and escape the rigidity of past and future, so we can finally enter the immeasurable intensity of all-encompassing simultaneity.

I prefer the first version.

I was at the movies earlier. Can't remember the title, but it was a boring film. Now I'm back at my desk with this heavy chain compelling me to craft something that can one day be put in print. I think I have only enjoyed one film in the last ten years. In fact, it was not the entire film. It was just a scene, the opening one. In my view, it is the finest twenty minutes in the history of cinema. I can't even remember the title of that film, and I haven't watched it in years. I believe it starts with an idyllic view of a countryside, where the man of the house is working outside while his daughters are hanging their laundry on a clothesline. At a distance, we watch two or three military cars driving on the road. A close-up of the father's face shows disconcertment. The cars come up to the property. They are Nazis. The bunch is headed by a well-dressed, dignified individual. After a few cordial remarks, the leader asks the man of the house if he knows who he is. I think the man, a Frenchman, identifies him as the "Jew Hunter". What follows is one of the most subtle psychological portrayals of two characters who find themselves in a diametrically opposed power relationship. The Nazi official, jovial, well-mannered, offers kind remarks to the household he visits while initially displaying no anomalous reason for his visit, other than a standard survey of the region. The man of the house, in a position of submissive hospitality, answers all the questions posed to him with a stoic attitude. He is obviously hiding Jews on his property; they cower beneath the floorboards. As the exchange flourishes first in French and then in English, the tension rises to a point of unbearable absurdity—a sequence I love—when the Jew Hunter, after requesting permission to smoke inside, takes out an extravagant horn-shaped Calabash pipe. Through the extenuating pressure of the Nazi's words, the Frenchman eventually succumbs to reveal the location of the fugitives. The confession leads to the complete demoralization of the man as he watches the soldiers enter the house and fire round after round at the poor innocent victims through the wooden floors. A young woman escapes, running frantically, toward the horizon. For some undisclosed reason, the Jew Hunter abstains from shooting her down.

Did my memory serve me right there? Why am I wasting time writing about a film I can't even remember the title of? Was it an unconscious desire to check if I have a future as a film critic? Did I secretly desire to plumb the depths of a twenty-minute scene in just over three hundred words? Am I always to ask unanswerable questions? Let's move on before I cower beneath the shame of my inanity.

I can't recall the past as well as I can invent it. As a boy I remember being delusionally obsessed with absorbing the smallest details of all the objects in my house. It became a kind of game, looking at things with what must have been an idiotic stare, trying to capture all the shades, textures, imperfections of whatever thing was in front of my head. It started around the time I turned five. I had learnt to write the number 4 and had been practicing for months. All of the sudden, I had to learn how to draw this impossibly contorted dragon wing, the number 5. It was my first and earliest realization of the impermanence of life. How could I, a four-year-old, imperceptibly, so painlessly awake as a five-year-old after a placid night's sleep? Such an innocuous event catapulted forward this mania to remind myself constantly that all things shall pass. If I could change so effortlessly into a five-year-old, what other strange changes would happen around me? I wanted to secure clear memories of objects before they changed into something else. An apple, besides its tasty juice, was much more than a round shiny thing. Through detained attention to its surface, I could begin to see maps, hieroglyphs, deep space patterns, interlocked horizons from a hyperdimensional reality. I became immersed in the infinite contents of every detail. Of course, I didn't see those things when I was five. I can't even remember what I used to see in things. I can only recall getting lost in a maze of details. My parents began to worry: *Is he autistic?* I heard them say. When I entered school, I would spend hours studying the fissures on my desk. Or the rusty metal bars of my classmates' chairs. The window was always a magnet, not because of what was outside it, but because of the tones it would assume depending on the time of day; ghosts, angels, aliens seem to appear and dissipate with the greatest ease on that holographic plane. I was one of the last students to learn how to read and write; the texture of the paper was much more important than the words or pictures therein. This intensity of the minuscule impacted me in many other, much subtler ways. My memory started to misfire. While protecting every detail in the vault of my memory from the torrent of time, my mind started to disregard the cadence of the calendar. There were just unlimited details stored in my mind, but no chronology. Without the frame of time, there is just inexhaustible content. I had the hardest time explaining to my teachers what I had done during the weekend or telling my friends what I'd do for the holidays. I was losing grasp of the narrative that envelops the details of my life; there were just these limitless episodes, the entrancing curves of a string of smoke, a tornado of flying ants journeying around a volcano (motes of dust

below the living room lamp), the intricate vertebra (leaf vena-
tion) of ancient beasts (foliage) leaving their skeletons to rot
every autumn on the windswept sidewalks. Imagination went
on a rampage; I was ecstatic knowing I could pause any given
moment to unbox from a nearby object the elixir of bottomless
detail. It became a duty, because soon objects would dissolve
into something else, even into nothingness itself.

Weak, Slightly Contradictory
and Incredibly Subjective Philosophical Interlude I

*Premise: the past is liquid; the future is a crystalliza-
tion emerging from the featurelessness of the past.*

The past, through the catalyzing element of the
present, solidifies into the future. The past is the
ground on which we stand, but what is the past? From
the past I have only memories (oh, really?), that's
obvious enough. However, an arbitrary factor under-
mines any safe footing in the past: the interpretation
of those memories.

Because the past is a swampy ground in which I
can be forever sloshing through its lack of definite
form, getting lost in its murky air, confounded by its
shifting levels; by the time I make it to any present
moment, I am drenched in mud and mire. Here is the
first law we can proclaim, something a Phenomeno-
logical Newton would have penned: Every mental act
has an equal and opposite reaction. In short, my belief

in what has happened in the past is directly influencing how the future will be perceived. As complementary opposites, the future compensates for the mushy form of the past, by forging solid, clearly delineated surfaces, not unlike the rugged surface of a glacier.

Since I grew up without a clear sense of time, now the future is making up for my previous temporal laxity. Has my time-free past maimed me in the tangle of an inflexible future?

I can't know for certain what happened in my childhood years. My interpretation of my past keeps changing constantly: an accomplishment a year ago can easily become a failure today. The past is being reinvented as I go along. The ancient proverb "As above, so below" finds its temporal counterpart in: "As before, so not henceforth." The future is a fictitious growth arising from the unappeasable fluidity of the past. That's why I foresee the future as an uneventful, rigid routine. I have no certainty in my past, no interest in my future. This lack of imagination hinders me from picturing anything beyond the few present thoughts running through my mind. No surprise I can't string together a story-like narrative five pages long.

How can I ever write my *magnum opus* with this disability of mine?

I never get tired of my megalomania! I should have erased that preposterous question. Who am I to even have a minor classic to my name, much less a series of published works, out of which one is considered my *magnum opus*? I'm going to have many good laughs rereading this on my deathbed. If I can make it to old age, that is. I just finished a giant Toblerone bar, a delicious sugar high to complement the excitement I felt while writing my philosophical interlude. I'll look back at my mid-forties as the nascent period of intellectual puberty. Some reflective capacity exists, yet one remains deluded by the nonsensical pipe dreams the mind can conjure if left unchecked.

I can foresee genuine humility emerging one day, though. But for this to happen there must be an alchemical process in the mind, a slow grinding behind the scenes of perception. There will be a third eye looking at the rough cliff of life and my pathetic inability to climb it. It will declare: *I've tried my best but did not succeed… and that is fine.* I will smile when young people approach me to share their wild dreams of taming the world. Reality will always be a savage and we're nothing more than little hares hiding in cramped burrows, praying to whatever is in fashion that day (spirits, gods, mathematics, parallel universes) that we get a few more days, please don't get me flayed just yet, that if I get one or two more years, I'll become something, the world will be proud of me; pretty please, I'll show you my worth, just don't gorge me up yet. I'll smile, not condescendingly, but genuinely, knowing that there is no other way. I'll even listen, giving my fullest attention, as they describe their schemes and maneuvers to dodge the bullet. But deep down I'll know it will be in vain. It's part of the universal human cycle, to be born, desire, fail to get what you want, and when all strength is gone or time is up, accept your fate.

Frictionless activity. Effortless flow. That's what it's all about. The clouds have cleared. Crisp winter air, I can almost breathe in the blue. The last leaves of autumn crumple against the gutters. The cars glide by as if an invisible but orderly current carried their mother-of-pearl surfaces through the streets. Pedestrians, in multifarious fashion styles, roam like birds of paradise on a predator-free island. Thoughts, thoughts, and more thoughts, flowing carelessly through the empty receptacle of my mind. *There is no free will*, my friend would say. And I would add: *nothing to do, everything will happen by itself*. Allow the thought of death to arise. Let the correlating fear appear as a seamless consequence. Let the resistance to that fear come forth even when you think it is irrational to be anxious about an abstract future. Let the knowledge that everything is predestined be remembered or forgotten according to its own precious will. I can change nothing. Whatever is in charge here is not the invisible "I" behind phenomena. There is only a stream of images playing in the theater of life. Behind the image, there is nothing.

It's time to get more personal. Can't imagine anyone would ever like to read such interminable pseudo-intellectual ramble. My name is No, I can't. There is this stubbornness in me. I can't start talking transparently about myself. It is as if language, born pristine, baby-faced inside my head, gets mutilated, decrepit, and incurably complex once it touches the page. I would honestly like to weave dozens of pages of flowing narrative. But how, where does the inspiration come from to write a *Midnight's Children*? How can you conceive all these situations out of thin air? There must be an innate faculty few are born with to reach such dizzying storytelling heights. Or is it relentless practice, debugging your brain for years until it regurgitates the purest streams of language cleansed from the retarding rubbish of self-doubt?

> *little fireflies that flare up momentarily one evening before settling forever in the dark void of anonymity.*

My secret wish: if I write long enough, I will become somewhat decent. I want to achieve some sort of universality with my fiction. I envision clarity of language, paragraphs that can be read effortlessly while still generating explosive imagery in the mind of the reader. It must have depth while not being overly intellectual. It can be both poetic and philosophical, but not arrogant and didactic. I love a good metaphor, but I must resist this addiction to include one every second sentence. There must be a good story too. Something credible, nurtured in real life but released fully-fledged in the ethereal medium of fiction. A work that explores the limits of human personality, pushing those boundaries until an unforeseen transmutation, caused by the sheer irreversibility of the world's motion, forces the protagonist to trespass the bounds of sanity and to commit a terrible crime. Tenderness, rage, the cruelty of the world's indifference, the hope of rising above suffering. All these things must be in there, in a balanced and structured way. I need dialogues too. Besides a short dialogue I published in *Harvey's Review* (the editor-in-chief was a regular at a bar I worked in, and I got him smashed more than a few times on the house),

I don't think I have ever written more than a couple pages of dialogue in any other work. Was it really a dialogue? Perhaps it is a monologue in two voices.

Dialogue – the weather

-       Nobody in their right mind would want to lose the 'joy of life'.

-       I agree, but there are examples of incorrigible gloom, even of 'asphyxiating' despair, wouldn't you concur?

-       Surely. Remarkable how some people can wallow in their own misery for years and forgo that undeniable birthright to be wholesome and happy.

-       It's simple. Negativity seems to possess a 'magnetic' quality to it; a certain sweetness can be savored in that 'hole of darkness', if you know what I mean.

-       Why on earth would you choose the 'swampy foulness' of depression when you have the 'golden light' of happiness within your reach?

- My friend, dark forces loom over the psyche! Conflicts that are not totally under our control.

- So, the person is not held account-able, and it is purely necessity that bounds him or her to the 'pit of depression'?

- I think it can best be explained through an allegory.

- You mean, like a myth?

- More of an analogy. Imagine the 'in-evitability of death' embodied as bats that constantly fly above a traveler's head, the 'futility of achievements' as a thick fog that surrounds the landscape and the 'self-ishness of others' as an endless jungle of thistle as far as the eye can see. As the traveler goes about his own life, perhaps glimpsing the 'towering mountains' of mys-tery at a distance or the 'radiating fount' of beauty that can be found in miscella-neous natural forms, he is deemed to 'bump into' those ugly facts of life every now and then.

-     But there are reasons to be happy, the mountains, the fountains of…

-     Yes, but as the traveler gets older and weary, he begins to spend less time 'on the road' and settles for a certain refuge along the way.

-     Does it have a nice view?

-     Occasionally, but it's a foggy country, infested with bats and unfit for leisurely walks because of the . . .

-     Thistles?

-     Dangers of the weather.

-     Typhoons?

-     The climate of his mind.

-     The sudden apparition of a mental disease?

-     A slow path to pathos.

-     Please elaborate.

-      The traveler acknowledges the 'boun-
ty' of his heritage and the 'fortune' of his
adventures but eventually reaches a standstill. A 'thick overcast sky' eclipses his
perception of joy.

-      A devil's trick?

-      Or a mind's tic.

-      A sinful habit?

-      A colorless habitat, I would say. The
traveler settles in the 'domain of boredom'. He feels the 'edge of wonder' has
grown blunt and there is little left in the
'barrel of surprise'.

-      But he's prejudiced; he hasn't tra-
versed the whole of 'life's adventure'.

-      Perhaps, but his very ability to
foresee his well-being depends on his experience of what's gone before. As more of
'the same' keeps happening in his life, he
deduces - ipso facto - that nothing new can
emerge.

-     So, he settles for a monotonous life?

-     He projects into the future and calcu-
lates.

-     And what would be his purpose?

-     That very question, the settling of
his uncertainty.

-     Seems like entering a spiral labyrinth.

-     Certainly; and the uncertainty of the
search allows him to comfortably —albeit
sorrowfully— 'lean back' against the 'hard
mount' of reality.

-     How can you find comfort in frustration?

-     You start 'scratching' the walls of
your prison. You accept your shackles and
dedicate yourself to the 'enclosed area' of
your fate.

-     Have you always carried this 'heavy'
philosophy with you?

-     I'm no philosopher, I'm merely describing what I see in others around me. I
am a truthful reporter of the 'loneliness'
of the human condition.

-     But at this stage in history, with
hindsight, we are aware of the new 'human
potential'. How can some souls give up the
'quest for perfection'?

-     Knowledge has gone sterile no matter how cogently its message is formulated.
There is no 'spice' left in it to 'stir up'
an appetite, if you know what I mean.

-     But we have overcome the hardest part.
We can glimpse, finally, an end to all this
suffering. People must just try.

-     The 'fabric' of their resilience has
been punctured by too many defeats.

-     So, they will give up even as we see
on the horizon 'the end of our troubles'?

-     The keenest intelligence is aware of
its limits, our psyche is not immune to de-
ception, and the brutal exigencies of society are too much for the mind to bear while

still maintaining its sanity; they eventually 'erode' away the 'pedestal of reason'.

- So only a select few will 'cross over' this epoch into the 'new age of bliss'?

- Only a few lucky ones; I don't think so much rapture can be endured by the masses.

- But that potential is codified in our being. Savants of science have confirmed this.

- Yes. They have finally proven that human beings have the ability to 'cling to' and 'harness' their highest state.

- And we now know what that is!

- On the contrary. Science is unable to determine what that value is. It will depend on the embedded cultural values of those that reach the 'apex of humanity,' as they call it.

- Do you see the emergence of a 'totalitarianism of the heart'?

—   Something much stranger and inexpress-
ible…

Maybe I should desist from that dream of writing universal fiction. Is there such a thing? I should stop resisting my
impulses and give free rein to my style. Who honestly under-
stands half of what Pynchon is writing? Isn't *Ulysses* a work
skirting on the brink of unintelligibility? They are masters no
doubt, but can we, neophytes in the lost art of obnubilating
language, produce lesser works that could one day demand a
little bit of respect?

Can language evolve consciously? Can a genius of the stature of Joyce have the ability and influence to transport the English language to a new plane, creating, so to speak, the next
floor in the tower of Babel? Unlike the original one, which
was created once and then discontinued, this would be a living tower, a constant creation and evolution, the willed transmutation of speech by prodigious architects of language, as
we—the slaves of their language—journey through history,
keep building higher and higher by following their guidance,
until the day comes when we are all the serfs of sound, having
completely lost sight of the floors below, of the ground, of the
foundational crude moans from which it all emerged? Or is it
blind happenstance, random accidents in the application of
language that must be endured for a century or two, silly me-
mes that take root in the mind, modifying the way we speak
and interact, pushed forth by any Joe or Josephine, pressing us
forward in that sightless path toward some incomprehensible
language our descendants will one day speak?

So, what is the issue with the above? The ideas are not terribly unoriginal. There is some meat in there. The issue is that I don't take the time to calmly assemble the medium through which the idea will be presented. I cannot repress my logorrhea. Instead, I should take an hour to write that paragraph above, rehearsing each step, so the sentence can effortlessly and elegantly waltz into the reader's mind.

THE ANATOMY OF EVERY OTHER MONDAY:

I wake up at 5AM to the second or third cry of my son. I've slept less than two hours. Brain fog. I immediately pick up my phone and check for new emails. No fan mail. No accepted submissions. I take the boy to the adjacent room to fetch a pair of socks. Deal with his fuss over not wanting to put his socks on. Let's go to the toilet to pee. You first and then me. Wash your hands. Find a book while I prepare breakfast. Oatmeal. By 8AM we're ready for kindergarten. I bike 20 minutes and drop him off. Brain fog. I wave good-bye through the window and won't see him until the following week's weekend. Cycle back home. At 8:56AM, boil water for coffee. Read a page or two while doing #2. Take a few deep breaths. Go to the kitchen and eat a croissant. With Nutella. I open my notebook to write a keyword. It can take a minute, maybe twenty, if I'm not distracted by my appetite. Often two croissants. With Nutella and a dash of sugar crystals. I write down my keyword. Let's say it was *Laughter*. Brain fog. 9.42AM, nap time. I wake up around noon. A blurry stream of hours passes by. At the end of the day, precisely midnight, I'll lock the furry collar around my neck and dive deep into an automatic writing session for no less than 180 minutes.

Was that an honest portrayal or just a reductionist contrivance, a fictional interpretation of what really goes on following the weekend when I've been with my son? I think there is one indisputable truth in that piece: brain fog. Would it be metaphorically or literally speaking? There's my brain and whatever is going inside it is adrift, lost in the murk of exhaustion and defeat. Will I ever be a good father, or will my son always remember me as the dad that had to give up and sleep his days away? Oh, there is a second fundamental truth there: Nutella. Not always croissants, but there is always a trace of Nutella at some point in my mornings, afternoons or evenings. What about automatic writing, have I ever practiced that? I had one piece written quickly in a flash. Flash fiction with no punctuation, an outpouring of deranged ideas not unlike the fiery speeches the Midnight Sun would deliver in his most inspired moments. It was rejected by most journals I submitted to, but I passed it around among my friends. One of them was an intern for an up-and-coming literary journal, and she polished it by adding punctuation and a title: "The One."

"Modernity must be seen as the application of an elegant but deceiving method, the systematic subjugation of consciousness to a very precise form of sustained hallucination. Language itself has been coded, since time immemorial, not only to preserve the fiction of the mind, but also to reproduce and expand its breadth. Today we no longer have any premise that is beyond the reach of doubt, with every value, aspiration and purpose engulfed by the liquid frontiers of our delusions."

I became aware of three things simultaneously occupying my mind, as he finished talking about our delusions. First, I was running out of beer, two, there was a punk, beautifully round shaved head, and deep black eyeliner, standing not far at the other end of the bar, while three, I was in the presence of The One, à la matrix.

He continued:

"Choice, decisions, freedom; these are myths that fuel our conditioning. The recognition that every event is predetermined is the only means to reach a slight degree of control; that alone can determine the outcome of your internal interpretation of the Event. You cannot forge that belief, it will be made unconsciously, perhaps even reluctantly, but once established, it will dye your worldview with its essence and aura. So today, at the edge of madness, we have one opportunity to reframe our predicament. Is it a nightmare? Or with luck, can we turn this miasma of sensation and confusion into nothing more than the soft flow of an innocuous dream?"

My beer finished, I signaled for another, the punk girl was getting closer, and we maintained eye contact for several seconds. The One, madly inspired, continued his speech as we approached midnight:

"To reach the denouement of this factitious drama one must become as vulnerable as possible, to be naked, so to speak, in front of the violent fire of the Lie. Endure with courage the streams of pain that will flood the mind. You will soon realize there is nothing there that can burn, and the fire eventually gives up its blaze in the vacuum that is our real self."

Beer was flowing, the girl was just behind me, slowly rubbing her rump against mine, the eyes of The One wild with theory and poetry:

"The Answer will not produce a sensation, will not relieve the ache, it cannot quench the fiery nausea of our philosophies. If an Answer is at hand, it will only be recognized by its absence of substance, its intangible voice coated in what necessarily must be a protective layer of silence. How does one attain the Answer? One must come to prefer not to know. You must abandon the knowledge of the knower. The scope of the hallucination is inconceivably large, as immeasurable as it is stubborn. It is a sea of phantasmagoria that reaches below the horizon of perception to encompass the totality of our being. Do not try to find firm land, do not swim against the currents, do not resist its tugs and pulls; allow its revolting mirage to suffocate you… drink and drown in its thick illusion."

Amen, I said. I had drunk too many beers by then, I bid farewell to The One as I took the punk girl in my arms, sweat and euphoria shining on my face; sometime around midnight I was to drown, like a good hedonist, in the thick shadows of her cave.

A one-dimensional storyline. A guy getting lucky while listening to an aberration of abstraction from a stranger at a bar. What is it that gives me pleasure in sounding like some sort of raving prophet high on hallucinogens?

It is possible that my biggest weakest is not taking this style to its furthest limits. Go beyond the schizophrenic inspiration of Dylan's *Tarantula*, the palpable madness of Burroughs. A supraconscious juxtaposition of the most dissimilar impulses, crafted after a painstakingly thorough process of eradicating the most natural associations that come between subject and predicate, time and place, emotion and concept, subjectivity and objective reality; everything ripe with sexual strife. Let's try:

Ferdinand, the echo of the cat, went planting into matter the laughter mother left colossal in the fridge. Massage this error. Mystery has many entrances into death, Swiss cheese but odorless, a classroom whose goats are chewing on the physics of the future. Science fiction settles as dust over the mirror of creation. No limits. My pet Ferdin and the duck we fed him, while the seductress drives the hour to arrive before my priapic marathon. Did you hear about the story of the physicist's cat? The newspapers laced with ribbons blink while the softest curve of womanhood is unveiled like a bastard sensation. Why has father collided with the moon but keeps polishing the toilet? Master fluids inseminate a catastrophe, a systematic union of desire and fate. Nietzsche invented rubber, blowing balloons in the first German zoo. Feeling like a zeppelin, nitrous oxide gamboling through those thin veins of despair, the man above it all—not only petty humans, but animals, the ants that will one day erect a

tower for dusk to swallow us whole. These
notes were found on a Tuesday morning inside the suite apartment belonging to the
prime minister of the royal salts. Classi-
fied and once set to music by Brian Eno, the
mirage of history is now being disputed as
the simulacrum we generate when we study
the adverts silence has, on primetime TV,
sublimated into a rendition of Christopher
Columbus' heart-wrenching confession of his
great regret in leading the way of the so-
called uber-mensch—who sadly is now Nar-
cissus about to drown in a pool of his own
tears—to a society that danced like tame
flames under the empire of an eternal jungle. Doors revolting, columns Corinthian,
arpeggio and the lyrical awe of calculus,
every magistral curve hardened into the
Flammenschwert of capitalism, the highest
echelon of civilization, pleasure—press the
button in the final climax now available:
suicide. Death opens like a rose, besides
the mountain is a fiction, the quagmire of
trauma builds the muscle of the hummingbird
howling with its infinitesimally small beak
into the last pocket of hope; the spot, cal-
loused, bruised, nearly catatonic, of the
human heart. It is often film, the waves
of creation crashing against the frames of

time. Tidy up the drama. The blame, a curl of wool around the neck of the first machine. Each slab of time, horizontally placed, sandwiching the pickles of memory, the mayo of truth, leave out the pepper of the combinatorial explosion, under the weight the layers become pure fluidity, with no fingers, stumps as archetypes to lift the meal of the day, all of history, liquified approaching the mouth, the gate where language will asphyxiate you as you drown in doom, one delicious sip of nothingness.

I lack genius. Take that sentence, it is dying. There is no humor in my writings. What cosmic miracle has allowed me to publish three novels? Two, really. The last one never left the printers. I keep going over the improbability of my career. A writer with nothing fundamentally valuable to share. Just some loosely assembled vignettes from my rambling mind, often disjointed stream-of-consciousness pantomime that nobody would care to decipher. No living soul could find any value here. At one point, I dreamt of imitating the greats—Pynchon, Cortázar, Nabokov—but I did not write a single page worthy of comparison. I published my first two books in a state of intellectual constipation. I had to restrict language to its bare essentials, so, I turned to my lesser greats. Camus, Orwell, Hemingway, and a few other US-Americans. I stopped calling them Americans long ago. I am American but I am not a citizen of the United States of America. America is an entire continent. Imagine a Frenchman proclaiming their national identity as European, to the exclusion of all other Europeans. Here in Europe, we tread in the steps of *Marianne*. We Europeans believe in the *Tricolore*. Europe is the land of wine. But I digress. So, I started devouring writers that employ simple prose, but it didn't help. Complex, rhapsodic, and often incomprehensible sentences keep my prose as clean as a kitchen rag. I couldn't believe my eyes when Nord Dam accepted my first manuscript. The founder is an old acquaintance of mine, but Iphrey—that pedantic louse who refers to himself as The Editor everywhere he goes—could just as well have rejected my contemptible attempts at becoming a published novelist.

The first novel, a novella in my eyes, consists of describing a room. A person, undefined gender, (though clearly any versed reader could denude my prose to reveal a John Thomas inside my protagonist's pants), studies a room the day before he is going to die. The character is not aware he is soon to die. We, the readers, are, so I tried to impregnate each detail with total meaning since it was the last time this person would ever encounter the things in the room, a weak metaphor for the limitations of our enclosed existence. My grand debut was, after a long unimaginative period looking for a best-selling title, titled *The Room*. Despite being a tiresome read and with few people reading it through, the first edition sold out. The success of the book stemmed from the considerable hype generated by two reviewers in a prominent daily newspaper and in a lesser known, yet critically authoritative, literary magazine. I was recognized as a forerunner in the emerging trend of Detailism, a movement that as the name suggests, focuses on the small details of our lives, rather than the grand narratives the "despotic" past has shackled us with.

Under the illusion of crafting a new chapter in literary history, I decided to keep writing more of the same. My second novel, also a novella if you ask me, was titled *Things*; a condensed, uninspired echo of the rebellious call to dismantle the "overbearing" stature of literature. I continued writing about things in the most mundane way, the way they look, feel or behave; casting aside any semblance of plot in favor of a drifting Bachelardian space, with deliberate indifference to any principle that can explain the ebb and flow of objects as they enter and leave our perception. If there are readers that enjoy this cacophony of abstruseness, a fourth book cannot be ruled out.

The third one, which was never released to the world, is titled *The Life of Objects*. It's not life as we'd normally define it. It's a non-linear narration of things as they exist of their own accord. In the book, purpose is superfluous, geography is irrelevant; it's a portrayal, in sparse poetic language, of the natural indifference objects exhibit to our attention or inattention to them, appearing and vanishing as they do at random, as if below the skin of the world were a giant current of nothingness that creeps in and out the horizon of perception to reveal things that are and certainly will be nothing. Reread that last sentence. Another testament to my impenetrable babble.

There, I am practicing by discarding, by purifying. Is it any good? Mother called last night; dad keeps appearing in her dreams. My late father's leitmotiv: the unbearable insistence of his being. In her dreams he is there in our house, doing the things he would always do. Always poking around other people's business. Listening in to what others are saying as he's piling up the firewood, polishing *plátano* leaves, removing cobwebs from the ceiling, feeding the cats. In her dream last night, he was cleaning the toilet while she waited for him to be done so she could pee. He keeps spraying vinegar on the toilet seat, on the floor, on the flush handle; meanwhile she's there holding herself for what seems like half a day, until she reaches a point she can no longer hold her anger (and urine) and spouts: The Bathroom Is Clean Alright, You Haven't Used It for Ten Months, It's Been Free Of Man-Pee OK! My father retorts: You should not wait until the last minute to come to the bathroom. Always happy to hurl a smart reproach. She wakes up the moment her pajamas start to swell with the warm stream of her urine. Ma, I say, do you see the symbolism there. He is simultaneously erasing while preserving himself in your psyche, as annoying as he was, pestering you with his intrusive presence (pee). Your mind is both trying to honor and release him, and you feel you are not in control, you are holding back; but your body aches for a discharge, the cataract of grief is on its way.

under the weight the layers become pure
fluidity, with no fingers, stumps as archetypes to lift the meal of the day, all of
history, liquified approaching the mouth,
the gate where language will asphyxiate you
as you drown in doom, one delicious sip of
nothingness. The leopards are rich, realize the soliloquy of fur, the origins of

architecture began with the way we dressed when still animals; nature's fashion the Ur-Mother of city layouts, the shape of temples, the maze of pipes, the solace of parks & fountains, Earth clad in the Anthropocene, materialistic dervishes spinning out of control, our greed is Velcro amassing rubbish to her thighs, petrol stains under her fingernails, carcasses in the millions in her armpits, dizzying fumes clouding her vagina, her nude landscapes now befouled by concrete bristles that house the pulsating discontent of the genius germ.

What do I really want? Let me imagine that I'm about to die in a week's time. No more bullshit. Can't dream of writing a masterpiece. Even if I did whip out a little classic, what's it worth? How relevant will it be when our species is scavenging for bone marrow through the desolate corridors of a wasted civilization, long after I've been reduced to dust. Or even if civilization flourishes and transcends our self-centered mode of life, by then they'll be speaking a cyborg language, a labyrinthine math-speech that will scoff at our primitive semantics. Even before my imminent death I should already come to terms with the futility of my ambition. What do I really want, below all this pretending? Can I lower my defenses, drop all this pretense, this hard-boiled intellectualism that borders on lunacy, and come clean, vulnerable like the reject I am, unarmed without philosophical nomenclature, a meek, thesaurus-free individual that's all kitsch inside, gooey like a twelve-year-old in love with his math teacher? Let's try.

My high school friends attempt to persuade me to do sports after school. To go to the arcades. I don't find the energy for that. I am suffering. Life beats me constantly. I can't even identify the problem. I can't tell my counselor what I want. He says it's normal to feel uncertainty. That's it, uncertainty is a magnet. Negative emotions come rushing into that center of not knowing what's what. I am trying daily to overcome my depression. I am reading self-help books. Positive thinking. The problem is in the mind. Can the mind change itself, lift itself from its own bootstraps? Impossible; there's no free lunch, I learnt that in math class. My math teacher is gorgeous. I study her face every day. The way those lips move as she explains algebra, her sweet voice as she says: Pythagorean. I feel funny inside when she talks about triangles. Especially isosceles. I feel a swelling in my pants. My friends asked if I've tried caressing the obelisk. It sounds as confusing as it is appealing. I'm not very good at math or biology. I like to draw eerie patterns. Can't do portraits. Just wiggles, spirals within

spirals. I get lost doodling in class. My
entire notebook is filled with these maz-
es. Melissa is her name. She told us about
fractals the other day. I like the sound of
that, fractals. Endless parts of a whole
that keep repeating themselves, forever. At
home, my sister is going through a phase.
Won't talk to anyone. I stay quiet in my
room playing with the cats. Looking out the
window. The wind. The little speckles of
dust being free. I want to feel free. Like
nothing could hurt me. Float in the world
without a care or worry. That's what I want.
Freedom from the world.

Not good enough, not even for a twelve-year-old's prose.
I need to transcend the text. Write in a way that words become invisible. Prose as a transparent lens, leaving the real
substance of existence exposed. Text so perfectly discreet as
to vanish from view, leaving the mind's reader inside the juice
of pure living. A linguistic feat, a discursive *trompe-l'œil*, pregnant with the ache of lived experience. That's what I want,
to rear language as a bridge into reality, make fiction bore a
tunnel into the light of day, anchor the reader in a world as
palpable as the book they are holding in their hands. That is
the true mission here, the only oasis in the desert of impermanence. Feed our conceptual rivers into the crystalline blue of
tropical seas. Escape the text through language itself, to drill
with the sharpness of words into the core of being alive, here,

today, among eight billion human beings.

Ok, so I'm about to die, don't get derailed this time. What is it that I really want? I'm dying, I have nothing to prove. Don't need validation, honors, the Pulitzer. Don't need to come up with a fancy theory of literature, text transcending text, whatever that could mean. I need something more elemental. Whatever is at the core of time before it is veiled by the next eclipsing moment. I only have this axis, the point upon which everything revolves. The conditions outside are beyond my control. My feelings are out of my control. My body is functioning by itself. Everything is external. Even being aware I cannot switch on or off. Everything is given automatically, no effort or design needed. What do I want then, when the world is a whirlpool of phenomena revolving around a question mark?

It's just language. I'm not driving at anything serious. Playing with linguistic bubbles. I've had funny ideas about language for some time. I found this in my blog on a random November day, fifteen years ago:

There is an immeasurable
relativity like a
pendulum splitting the
fractions of words in an
infinitesimal curve in
the reception of
meaning.

M··········s, all Im
saying is that no single
word will ever be
understood. Every mind
interprets words
differently based on
their previous
experience ~~and~~

~~~~~~~~~~~~~ of that
word. Therefore any
statement, expression or
exclamation will be
forever (funereally)
buried in the vast chasm
of incomprehensibility
and incommunicability.
The language itself will
one day disappear and
~~~~~~~~~~~~~

these words here that
you seem to so aptly
understand will be
hieroglyphics for
creatures vastly
stranger than us. You
have therefore that
choice to pretend that
communication (and
therefore knowledge) has
a real existence or
submit to the invariable
prescription of madness:
we are ultimately alone
in our unique paradigm
and isolated from any
true understanding of
one another.

What does this entail
honeybunch?

Simply that we are free
wanderers and all is a
commendable illusion.

Good bye.

What poppycock from such a cocky wannabe guru. The first thing is that I'm not sure I've ever felt free, even after all my deliberations about the illusory nature of reality. I'm still stuck in the thick of it, no matter how intellectually solid an argument I can make in favor of its impermanence. So, I'm a hypocrite. Two, what's that pedantic attitude? Like I had all the answers. If anything, I mask my impotence with this veneer of intellectual control. That's why I dress impeccably. It's not a sign of strength, quite the opposite. Every morning I wake up like a bloated sack of bones, an embarrassing blob of squirming blubber, that pretends to hide, somewhere below those layers of gargantuan fat, a grain of uniqueness, a compressed diamond of talent, a sacred well of inspiration that makes me peculiarly special and entitles me to dress sharply while I look condescendingly at the toiling ants rollicking around me with smiles that only serve to broadcast their naiveté and gullibility in trusting the shadowy show presented on the surface of things. This is my biggest pretense, and I am ashamed of it. Long gone are the years I carried the meaning of meaning in my right-hand pocket, like the philosopher's stone, the ultimate get-out-of-jail-free card, the conviction that earthly pleasures are distractions from us seeing the unbearable reality: nothing will be remembered. The abyss has shrunk now, it's another shadow on the surface. Only our vain human intelligence can pretend to look deeper than the surface of things. I am today another ant, not yet smiling, but as foolable and artless as all the rest.

Also, I'm starting to sense a discrepancy in my thinking.

What ultimately exterminates the value of having a successful writing career?

Firstly, is it the view of a future when English is no longer a mainstream, or even an existent, language? The futility of writing is here dependent on the belief in a future, and that this future somehow bears more truth and import than our present moment. It is a flimsy argument because I ascribe more value to the imaginary than to present reality. A second underlying concern is that my writing will never reach a worldwide audience. So, I'm writing in isolation, my words are simply echoing within the walls of my cave. The third line of thought is that even if I achieve a level of recognition, I'm going to die. What is life at its core, beyond the veil of external validation? What is it that I seek while spending nighttime hours in front of a screen where, letter by letter, pages of dubious literary value are stored for no specific audience? Scribbling on sand while I wait for the tsunami of death to erase the last detail of my existence.

Boil it down to the essentials, you are worried about two tenets: Universality and Permanence.

One, Universality: There is an unconscious drive to attempt to reach a universal audience. The reality is that even if you are an extremely successful artist, you will only influence a very discreet section of the global community. The barriers of social class, evolving languages, culture, and ideology forever set trenches between the work and its attempt at universality; not to mention the sheer volume of new works being published every day—publishing a new book is as consequential as adding a hair to the back of a muskox.

Two, Permanence: Even if your achievements receive accolades, the positive reception of your work cannot be guaranteed in the future. The human psyche is a soup under constant modification by the age's preferred taste, regularly receiving different spices according to the *Zeitgeist*'s moral appetites, shifting from sweet Romanticism, to bitter Fin de siècle, to salty Social Realism, to sour post-holocaust Absurdism. And who knows what future *Weltanschauung* will condemn your creation as the wicked expression of a sick society deep in *Weltschmerz*, leaving one certain course of action: your work will be burnt—this being its greatest achievement—under a tower of your contemporaries' brightest works. End of story, period.

This is my poison, The Great Fatalism of my Thinking. The feeling of imprisonment within an open-ended life. The wind. The little speckles of dust being free. I want to feel free. Like nothing could hurt me. Float in the world without a care or worry. That's what I want. Freedom from the world. But if I allow a bit of self-criticism to step in, perhaps my mistake is in believing that I want to be omnipotent, to somehow transcend the possibility of failure, rather than embracing the messy ordeal of living and dying. Is it possible the opposite is the most desirable thing; rather than eclipsing the world, to be fully absorbed by it? To become a corpuscle in the gushing bloodstream of time, a single ineluctable note in the cacophony of creation, a blade of grass yielding to a wind's every desire, my mind wallowing within the steamy bowl of the cosmos. Being nothing more than a unified broth of mind and matter, indifferent to the inertial path leading this soup toward a gaping maw, the drooling orifice of nothingness, so eager to consume, with its unquenchable appetite, our newborn unification. It's 3:09AM, enough of this.

I am a happy man! Woke up to unbelievable news, *Things* is long listed for The Booker, The BOOKER! All these years of senseless efforts have deservedly paid off! My first course of action is to notify my former best friends. We're going to crack open champagne, I'll reserve a huge salon downtown, order tapas and the finest DJs, we'll dance, jump, howl, get divorced from the world as we deliriously squeeze the last sweet drops before dawn. This is the beginning of my real career. I'll begin publishing bi-annually. Traveling the length and breadth of US-America, lecturing, promoting books, meeting adorably young fans, watching from a 40th-story hotel room the spectacle of a dying civilization, while I, influencing the world's intelligentsia, begin to dream the next literary chapter in our collective search for meaning.

It's not the first time I've tried to picture some glorious event that could make me squeal in delight. No matter how many times I visualize or pen down that vision, it always comes off as trite and undesirable. What needs to happen before I can open my eyes one morning, without flinching, and whole-heartedly state, "I need nothing more." To write or not to write, to love or not to love, to eat or not to eat. A perpetual state of well-being, even in the clutch of anxiety and despair, to be wholly receptive to the tribulations a life will serve, alive and well as you stare at the end of the inverted tunnel, a tube of light with a point of approaching darkness at the very end.

I need a change of perspective.

He observes the color of the water as it travels down his swarthy skin. A low rumbling sound impregnates the air. The window gathers clusters of droplets, a slow unification that ends in rolling tears. But he is not gutted today. Light has a friendlier quality, the air sparkles with a freshness not experienced since childhood. His fingers begin to quiver with pleasure. Every surface of his body has the ecstasy of a blossom bud. The whirlpools by his feet make spiraling tunnels into the tender velocity upon which he now rides. Velvet rapture like moss over his entire skin. The snake makes a tongue in the cave of his mouth. Language, like an ancient fire, enters a trance around the vowel O. The eyes roll back into his head. Classifications become extinguished, as the hands caress the sheer beauty of the soap. Movement in the atmosphere translates into the binaural beats his ears attune to. The solidity of memories crumble into a flurry of ash. Matter becomes mother, embracing her lost only child. His heart begins to swell like an octopus, reaching out to touch each point of music that now lingers in the air. Straightened and now stiffening its tentacles it appears like a gigantic sea urchin united through countless filaments to each second of the cosmic clock, every node of time firmly orchestrating the beating of his organ of love. Juices like lava seeping from every pore, burning holes in the sky his mind now proceeds to enter. He is vanishing as quickly as he is being reborn. His walls falter, fail, fall. The room renounces its geometry. The sky gushes into his mind, distant thoughts accumulate into cumulus clouds in one beatific highway of mist and delirium. The azure is now scorched, and his swarthy skin is the column of the night. He climbs on his own. His speed augments as he circles around each sun. The emptiness of space dilates with his every breath. His body is beyond the limit of the known. His mind is equidistant from language and silence. Nothingness is just a frame he glides over. Love cannot encapsulate his awareness. He breaks to be-

come everything and nothing simultaneously. Night and day swing dizzyingly around a
single indivisible point. Time sleeps. He
is now free.

Transubstantiation would be the title of that. But I can't go
any further. The images escalate too quickly. Zero poetic re-
straint. Metaphors abound and lose touch with reality. Mul-
tiplication of images *ad nauseam*. This constant desire to step
out of language. No wonder I can never get beyond a page or
two in a new novel. I'll have hundreds of stillborn novels by
the time I die. The unbearable incompleteness of talent. Get
another job.

I've had to make ends meet through the acquisition of
menial jobs. Being broke had previously never been a worry
in my mind unless I couldn't afford a good-looking suit. A
vintage but high-quality zoot suit. I could make just enough
money for my nighttime drinks and a series of anachronistic
zoots; yes, I am overweight and need to rely on an eccentric
dandy look. Somehow, I always had enough for my petty ends.
That was until I became a father and money got sucked out
faster than it came in. I've had to put in long hours, but I didn't
mind it if I could read and write on the job. Security guard was
the easiest, especially the night shifts at the Grand Royal hotel.
I've spent so many nights there chugging down the delectable viscosity of Miller's crucifixion. Gosh his prose would turn
me on as I monitored the lobby while inebriated 50-year-old
foxes made their way to the elevator. Fantasies compounded
on fantasies. I think this is when I started to conceptualize

saucy short stories. Another temporary source of income. I poured my dissatisfied sex life into stories of losers getting laid by rich folk, in the classic mutually profitable exchange: The impecunious are always wild acrobats in the circus of life ready to share their zest for all, while the affluent, who are on the verge of suicide from the boredom of having every desire satiated upon command, seek a forbidden pleasure to release them from their monotony. *The Breasts of Wrath* was the result.

In the lobby of the Grand Royal hotel my dubious career as an erotic short story author started with a whimper. My first story was rejected by editors that made the open call for a new erotica section of the Sunday Queer edition (alongside a half-nude university student, the "9 boygirl" of the week). But they saw potential and gave me a prepayment for a 3-page story, if I kept it simple, with strong emphasis on the sex part (without being too explicit), and please please please avoid getting too "artsy". Somehow, I could construct basic storylines if sex was the focal point of the narrative.

About a certain kind of artist
(uncensored draft)

I then began to tell them how I broke my arm while trying to finish my latest work of art. I started by saying how the weather seemed unusually pleasant that day, the air was minty, slow currents of cool air refreshing the lungs and the sun out in the

wide blue without being excessively brilliant, making me feel elated & slightly
aroused for some reason. I was on my way to
the studio, thinking I would finally finish
that piece that had taken me so long to complete, when suddenly, without notice, I
stumbled upon an irresistible curl of perfume coming from a nearby passerby. I looked
around as I took deep breaths of that sweet
and nauseatingly sensuous fragrance. Where
was it coming from? I looked and saw, a few
paces away, a brunette walking slyly through
the crowd. That's her, I said out loud,
she's a raven. I continued speaking in au-
dible terms to passersby—to my own amazement and embarrassment. I pursued her for
two blocks and finally, after nearly crush-
ing a toddler on the way, caught up with her
at the corner of Reib*** street and Troo***
avenue, as we both waited for the pedestrian light to turn green. Ahem, I uttered, a
sound so clear and diaphanous, it could
have been the stark toll of a bell from a
nearby church. She did not seem to take note
of me, but I could now confirm that she was,
in fact, the source of that perfume so se-
ductively violent that it had distracted me
from finishing my long overdue piece of art.
You should be ashamed, I said, looking

straight at her rather opaque hair, and I
continued petulantly, how dare you distract
me from my existential duty? She turned and
looked at me, smiled and said nothing. I was
about to utter this sentence "you better
have a valid excuse to exude that perfume
into the general public" but I didn't because she was no she, but a gorgeous looking
40-year-plus man, with heavy eyeshade and
prosthetic moles—two in fact, one on the
left hemisphere of his face, above the cheek
and the other, slightly smaller, below the
right eye. He then said in a sweet, almost
inaudible, voice: "better to bleed roses
than suck the air out of somebody's dream".
I was stunned, what kind of person would
utter such nonsense, and yet, I could not
help being charmed by this incongruous
phrase. I stared, stupidly at first, at his
(or should I say their) thick fleshy lips and
then the voice, soft as dripping from their
lips, came again: "you are an artist, I pre-
sume". I said, yes; this time unhesitant,
too quickly perhaps, as they took a step
back and examined my clothes. "I don't deal
with artists", they said, then twisted their
torso to reach their red leather bag behind
their back, took out some lipstick simply
to secure the lid in place, returned it to

the bag and began crossing the street, a
millisecond before the light turned green
for us, but I stayed behind, perplexed and
satisfied—I had found it, I thought. I knew
now what was missing in my piece of art and
I quickly turned toward the studio to finish
it. At this point, I was poured another big
glass of wine at the party, I was interrupted then by the entrance of a philosophaster
that, upon entering a room, always greets
us with the cliché "why so gloomy, you pessimists?" I rolled my eyes and resumed telling the story to my acquaintances. So, I
continued, I reached the studio and as I was
opening the main door, the brunette ap-
peared behind me. I feigned surprise and
greeted them. What brings you here, I said,
as if not caring. They were tall, a handsome
person, with the right curves, flowing like
waves from their voluptuous body. "I want
to expose myself to you", they said, almost
in the same tone they might use to divulge
that I had something between my teeth. How,
I said, would you like to be exposed? They
smiled, their thin row of teeth peeked
through their robust lips and said nothing.
I took them in the studio, ripped their
dress off while my clothes made a momentary
tornado, swiftly tumbling across the room.

I fucked them. As I was getting dressed, I saw how their legs were blotched with patches of soft bleached-blonde hair that seemed like isolated palms in the white sands of their skin. Their thighs were taut like balloons with too much air, their male member hanged dripping intermittently very much like a faulty faucet. They got up nude as sunlight, unabashed, studying the works lying around. They stared at the work I was supposed to finish that day. "The color brown resembles a door that opens to what is truly black", dry and expressionless, their words hit me like crumpled balls of paper. You don't like it, I said, as I studied their proud buttocks, plump with muscle and curve. They stretched their arms and legs and stood motionless like a Vitruvian man in front of my work; "take me again", they said almost in a whisper. I came close and placed my hands flat against their back. I closed in and drew my arms around the ribs and reached for their breasts, softly pinching the nipples. "Harder you wimp" came a threat, as unexpected as provocative to my ears. I drew them away from the art piece and swirled them half-circle until our mouths made contact, one round cave wet with motion. Our eyes remained open, alert and menacing, like the gaze of two cruel predators certain of the same easy prey. They reached down and squeezed my balls. "Brown is merely a window in a sky that is becoming dark", a sentence I cannot, to this day, dissociate from pain. They held me for several minutes as I gasped for air, mercy, and orgasm. My cock had become so thick, with every pulse I could feel a stream of red electricity travel up and down my shaft. They finally released me, and I screamed with relief. I looked down at my testicles, now swollen with an unearthly blue-purple color, small trickles of blood from where their long nails had clung to my sack. I was suddenly overtaken by a type of euphoria; my breathing became hard and heavy, and I could feel in my whole body something like the raw lust that pervades throughout the animal kingdom. "Take me", they repeated, and I growled as I leaped toward them, grabbing first their exquisitely smooth penis, and coming closer, I bit them on the neck and tugged with determination as I began hearing their moans increasing in volume and rhythm until they became words. "Faster, faster". I didn't want them to come again just yet, so I made them turn and bend over as I quickly spat on

my hand and smeared my electric sword with
translucent saliva. With my left hand I
spread their buttocks and in one quick spear
throw I was inside them. I pulled their hair
close to my nose, those long locks of chest-
nut hair suffused with potent, insanely rich,
intoxicatingly sweet perfume. They had an
erection and began to masturbate as I kept
pounding hard. My two hands were firmly holding their shoulders and I pulled myself
harder and harder with every thrust. Strange-
ly I began getting dizzy, weak, and close to
fainting (maybe the fumes from the paints
were getting to me); but I just needed a few
more seconds for orgasm. I made a superhu-
man effort, grabbed their finely shaved scro-
tum while they pinched their ass harder and
we both exploded, ejaculating streams of
golden sperm all over the studio. At this
point of the story, the philosophaster mock-
ingly hit me on my right arm and tried to be
funny: "you're such a queer". Everybody
laughed, naturally I slugged down the last
of the wine in my glass. I knew then everybody there was of his type. I stared at him
for a second and tried to walk past him. He
stopped me and asked if I had read the latest book by the pseudo-art-critic Reu*****.
I didn't comment and walked on, he slurred

something I cannot recall. All I could think about was getting out of this crowd. I didn't have to deal with this phony and his class. I could now hit a bar and anonymously enjoy a few more glasses of wine. That night was terribly cold, smoke seemed to clot the city with a substance corrupt and cumulous. I entered the bar with the red neon sign near Holsma*** street. I ordered a glass of red from a slim frisky 20-year-old, clouded in mascara and tattoos. I was just about to discuss the details of the tattoo on her hand when they (now without makeup, wearing a masculine suit; the same unmistakable perfume however) interrupted me with a tap on my shoulder. I took a long breath in, while I felt my pants thickening with anticipation. The first thing they said was "what happened to your arm?"

That was it. A bizarre account of how an artist got laid. Déjà vu. The emptiness that I feel when I finish reading my own work could fill volumes of existential dread. It's no surprise when I consider it calmly. Following the untraceable lineage of past events leading to the present moment, through the steady but exponential fattening of fate, time has manufactured me (by chance or by design, I don't care) to be this person—let's put it bluntly: I've been configured to love literature. This love is my gift and my second poison. On the one hand, I have the seamless ability to enter the most outrageous narratives with a kind of childish ardor; my skeptical armor is dropped, and I enter the kingdom of fiction in rags, to be charmed by the lightest invitation into the mind-maze of another human being. For all my moaning, I am happy when I read. And the secret is clear: I forget myself but the fictional world, through magical contortions, is recast as a mirror for the real world, word pressed against world, the imaginary beaming a numinous light so we can discern and ultimately accept the darkness of the real without the weight of the self. If fate had stopped there, making me another avid reader, a bookshop assistant, a librarian, or at most a proofreader or translator, I could have led a content life. Naturally, the path to satisfaction is never without snarls. My second poison is no less than my desire to write. It could have come about in many ways and I'm probably one of thousands of living artists that never fulfill their nagging dreams. Countless literary idealists are out there who, after grueling attempts at forging the slightest semblance of a "classic", leave this world with huge yellowing manuscripts crumbled in their grandchildren's attics.

Weak and Frankly Incomprehensible
Philosophical Interlude III

The mind is a strange boat. Consciousness, like the waterway that carries the raft of the mind, is unfathomably deep. Inside the vessel of the mind, we carry all the things we know. We can start with the most

basic identifying features: our gender, age, societal position, etc. These ideas exist as narrative, the net we
throw into the water to catch our prey. In other words,
we throw a conceptual network into the world (isn't
the world only an appearance in our consciousness?)
and blindly hope that we will attain our objectives, the
fish of our desires. Deep in the middle of the night,
we retell each other our feats and failures, explaining that being such a type of person of such height of
such inclinations of such temperament of such talent
of such flaws of such ambition, we've been able to only
fish this kind of mackerel or that kind of calamari. We
tell ourselves, I'm a good tuna fisher. I'm a bad octopi
catcher. Our lullaby stories are only skimming the surface. The forces that operate deep down in the water
of consciousness cannot be translated into the simpli-
fied knots of our semantic net, so to speak. When I
tell myself I want to be a great writer, that the entire
concatenation of past events led me to have this irre-
ducible desire, I am fooling myself. There are other
stronger forces at play here, motives we haven't even
been able to name or label, unconscious subatomic
indefinable pulls that determine everyone's character.
All these pathetic attempts at conceptualizing the flow,
framing the currents, studying the surface of the water, in order to believe I can grasp what the sea does,
what it means for my livelihood, where it will lead me
should I remain steadfast to my allotted fishing skills,
are nothing but fanciful chimeras. One day you see

an unfamiliar thing floating in the water. A carcass of unknown origin, bloated like a prehistoric fish. As you inspect it you will know it is *Mystery* itself. From that day you start to question this watery world. You can't sleep at night as the water rocks your boat relentlessly to and fro. Then dawn arrives, perhaps it is the angle of the sun, or the eeriness of the dying moonlight, whatever made you look at the water differently, diffidently for an instant, that's when you realize you are floating in a sea of fiction, that you are only angling on a surface, which provides no clues of the depths that ultimately sway you.

3:03AM, I have a bruise around my neck after wrestling with my collar for twenty minutes trying to escape tonight from my existential duty. Now, I feel like my toes are speaking, their multiple lips in constant glossolalia. My eyes glide down to become nipples wide awake. Armpits erupt like feverish sea anemone, with tentacles in total disarray. My lips turn to hardened crust, the tip of the chimney spewing the smoke of my anxiety. My navel sinks deeper into my gut, I feel the fabric of the intestines warp under the extreme pressure. The spacetime of my hunger is torn as the black hole of my birth scar bores a passageway through my organs. This infinite tunnel has me impaled to the bed, impossibly heavy as a giant slab of granite at the foundation of the universe. My hands are now ideas gesticulating, in a wild bee-dance, the hidden pleasures of my ignorance. My toenails root out any assumptions still lingering in my disassociated mind. I sense my feet breathe in large volumes of air; my new lungs begin to lift me up from the unmoving ground of being, time breaks like a crystal film above me, I gain momentum as I plunge into myriad hours, events everywhere shimmer as the shattered incongruous pieces of time, every sharp moment piercing my skin. I feel cramped in a single minute, my voice trapped in the space of a millisecond. Without warning, organs begin to return to their original location, ideas become ethereal, hands become instruments to take hold of the tangible world, my feet impel me to get up and open the window. I'm back in my room.

I must be overworked, at night my brain is finally ... submerging in a vast metaphysical lake.

If I must be sincere, I've always believed people spoke games, nothing but airy forms of play. For all its rigid rules and agreements, language—it seems to me—is nothing but a random stitching of words, like a child placing all sorts of miscellaneous objects into a mini-geyser just to see the clutter spring into the air in the most unpredictable, abstract patterns. I've been writing without any serious purpose. Not to become a writer, as I like to fool myself at times, but to serve as a sort of Turing machine that can string together—on my most inspired days—a sequence of poetic forms that will inform people of their powerlessness, of the mind's unswerving compulsion to create meaning and, to some degree, beauty, from the random symbolic patterns that surround them.

I can't control the origins that control me. That sentence captures the absence of free will concisely. If I cannot control, influence or modify the preconditions of my being, how am I going to exert my free will now? But I'm not here to convince anyone about anything, at most I'd only be stirring people's already existing biases. Who could be conceited enough to think that they can persuade the masses through written language; if anything, they are accentuating innate and unconscious tendencies ready to manifest in the public sphere. I'm not here to prove to people that they are or aren't free. I am just a manufacturer of text and whoever ends up reading this will be giving it all the meaning they want to see in it. If you want to see a squashed banana on this page, that's up to you.

There is plenty of resistance in people when they hear everything is predetermined. It's not their fault. The die is cast, nothing can be changed, not even the angry thoughts or the feelings of disgust that arise after hearing this idea. I don't think it matters much. Thoughts are being generated constantly without any assistance from "us". A thought, any thought, appears out of the blue. That very instant, you believe whatever the thought is suggesting. Take, for example, the thought of doubting what you think. Just by having that thought in your head, the suggestion arises that you should doubt your very thinking. Without the initial thought about doubting your thoughts, where's the doubt going to come from? The quality of thought dominates the experience of any given moment. (Am I turning New-Agey?)

The trouble of not having free will comes from the belief that you are an autonomous agent who is orchestrating the events of your life. Sure, most people will easily admit that there are forces stronger than our will. I've spoken to people with all kinds of beliefs. Catholics, Sufis, Atheists, Pantheists, Swamis, Jews, Mindfulness Practitioners, Agnostics, Materialists, Communists, Mormons, Sikhs, Anarchists, TM devotees, Simulationists, Advaita Vedanta enthusiasts, Solipsists, Cynics, Pessimists, *et alia*. Regardless of their belief system, most will agree with the popularized AA prayer: *Grant me the serenity to accept the things I cannot change, courage to change the things I can, and wisdom to know the difference.* You see, somewhere deep down, people believe that they have a modicum of power to influence the course of world events. You challenge this view, and they feel offended. It's nothing but a misunderstanding, coming from the same involuntary thought stream that informs all other aspects of their life: that they are an independent living self. It is not just a thought; it is an essence carried by every thought. Each thought implies that existence of that independent living self. Take away this individualistic essence from the thoughts and our experience is just a field of movement, feelings, sensations, actions; an emptiness not unlike the sky hosting any visiting cloud, bird, airplane, the occasional helium balloon that slipped away from a child's hand. Since we can't control the thoughts that arise and our thinking implies an agent behind the thoughts, we will continue to think we exist as agents responsible for the course of *"our"* lives.

ACT I

Setting: English pub, with seven to
eight wooden tables and chairs. Scarce
clientele. In the center, two middle-aged
adult males sit in intimate conversation.

A half-way burnt white stearin candle is
lit, its flame quivering in the stuffy damp
air. A screen shows a football match, fans
celebrating.

                    JAKOB
               (introspective)

     It was meant to be.

                    PAUL
                 (gloomily)

     As if written in the stars.

                    JAKOB
                  (sighing)

     It couldn't have ended any other way.

                    PAUL

     It is the last game of his career, and
     he's got it, the highest glory.

                    JAKOB
             (Eyes moist with emotion)

     The game will never be the same.

(SILENCE - except for the wild cheering
from the TV screen, a player is being in-
terviewed)

JAKOB
(with an involuntary stutter)

I thought I would be happy witnessing
this. It's like, almost as if, I… kinda
sense… I… I feel a deep sense of… emptiness.

PAUL

I feel numb inside.

JAKOB

Yes, it's like watching a film you've
seen a hundred times.

PAUL

Feel like it was all scripted and played
out exactly as expected.

JAKOB
(making sure he was heard)

     Yes, it's like watching a film you've
seen a hundred times.
                    PAUL

The best player of all time, winning the
World Cup, on his final game.

                    JAKOB
     (looking at the ceiling, as if in deep
                    prayer)

Why are some born to succeed, while others are doomed to failure?

                    PAUL

We'll never amount to anything.

                    JAKOB

     A couple of idealists, never fulfilling
their potential.

                    PAUL

A couple of barely formed pearls no one
will ever discover.

                    JAKOB

  A couple of barley stems that will never
develop their kernels.

                    PAUL

We'll wither before we can metamorphose
into a delicious glass of beer.

                    JAKOB

  No one will ever produce our screen-
plays.

                    PAUL

Two writers penning ideas for the rubbish
bin.

                    JAKOB

  Two screenwriter wannabes.

                    PAUL

Forever in the shadows of Tarantino and
Kaufman.

JAKOB
(rubbing his face with both hands)

Two more wasted human lives.

PAUL

I'm not superstitious, but after today, I
have this new sense that everything moves
through a single course.

JAKOB

The river of history.

PAUL

The creek of time.

JAKOB

The canal of choicelessness.

PAUL

The ditch of fate.

(The friends stare at each other's faces, goggle-eyed as if in disbelief)

                    JAKOB
        (reaching for Paul's ear, murmuring -
                  barely audible)

        I can't take it anymore.

                    PAUL
        (face turning red, a sudden eruption of
                    anger)

We're in prison.

                    JAKOB
        (about to get up from the chair)

Our days are scripted.

                    PAUL
        (raising his voice)

We're trapped in the jaws of destiny!

        (JAKOB about to walk away)

                    PAUL
        (in dismay)

Where are you going?

                    JAKOB
        (nervously looking around, half-standing,
                half-sitting down)

        I'm feeling queasy.

                    PAUL

        What's the matter?

                    JAKOB

        I can barely feel my body.

                    PAUL
            (motioning with his hands)

        Sit down, take a deep breath.

                    JAKOB
            (after a moment's pause)

        I've just had a revelation.

                    PAUL
        (leaning in while anxiously checking no
                one is listening in)

        What? Tell me!

                    JAKOB

The ultimate irony of fate!

                    PAUL

What is it?

                    JAKOB

We're characters in a script.

                    PAUL

Are you being serious?

                    JAKOB

Listen, just think about everything that's
happened up until now. We've been working
together for years trying to create the next
sensational series, a blend of edgy philosophy with enough juicy content to keep the
masses tuned in. We often attempt to write
about new perspectives of time. Synchronicities, parallel life tunnels, prophecies
being fulfilled. Did you watch that game
carefully? It was perfectly planned. The

                    92

GOAT was about to easily achieve his last
and final taste of glory, only to be detoured
by two late goals by the opponent. Our hero
comes to the fore during extra time with a
messy convoluted goal, only to be denied
by a last-minute equalizer. The penalties
went on for a total of 12 rounds per team,
with the first penalty missed by the GOAT,
only for him to score on his second attempt
to win the final. What were his words after
winning it: I wanted this for so long, before the tournament began, I had a feeling
this was the one. Remember our last rejected screenplay? A precocious teenager with
the gift of telepathy can foresee events in
the future…

PAUL

Yes, yes. I see the parallels. Maybe it's
just a coincidence.

JAKOB

  It is not. At the end, the teenager looks into the future to see these two
post-material beings discussing the pattern of earthly existence…

                        PAUL

Yes, yes. They begin a loose philosophical
discussion about how they...

                        JAKOB

  Despite all their powers, wisdom and
freedom, they know they cannot do otherwise. What binds earthly life, binds the
metaphysical realm.

                        PAUL

What are you trying to get at?

                        JAKOB

  We are in an Escher drawing.

                        PAUL
                  (in exasperation)

Have you gone mad?

                        JAKOB
                 (raising his voice)

  We are nested in an infinite Matryoshka
doll.

                    PAUL
            (pleading with his hands)

Bring it down a notch, will ya?

                   JAKOB

Every single word we utter has been
scripted. Every action preordained. Every
moment is an endless reproduction of the
original pattern.

                    PAUL
        (clearly relaxing his skepticism)

Like a Mandelbrot set?

                   JAKOB

   Bingo!

                    PAUL
    (very slowly articulating every syllable,
                sarcastically)

E... ve... ry... word... has... been... scrip...ted.

                    JAKOB

Everything… from the beginning of time.

    (SILENCE — except for chairs moving, in-
distinct chatter from a corner)

                    PAUL
    (after a period of deep introspection,
        shrieks in a sudden start)

AHA!

                    JAKOB
(startled, nearly falling backwards on his
                  chair)

    What?!

                    PAUL
    (coming closer to JAKOB)

There is an escape!

                    JAKOB

    No, everything, EVERYTHING is already
set.

                         PAUL
                 (staring intensely at JAKOB)

Listen closely. We've become aware of the
inevitable.

                        JAKOB
                 (with a disquieted look)

  Not following.

                         PAUL
                 (coming closer to JAKOB)

In our minds, we KNOW every moment is
planned. This knowledge sits next to each
event. It influences the future. It is our
freedom. Just watch…

  (PAUL gets up and begins to shake and
wiggle his body violently. Total chaos to
his movement, no pattern or rhythm detect-
ed)

You see, it's working already. I wouldn't
have done that without the knowledge of
your

(Using index and middle fingers to air
quote the word)

'revelation'.

JAKOB
(with a smirk)

Now you've gone mad!

PAUL

I'm dead serious. I think you are right…
it is scripted, until we came along! Watch
this!

(PAUL repeatedly taps the table as if
it were a drum, then turns around to howl
like wolf)

(Voice of the bartender - unseen - from
the back of the stage)

Keep it down over there!

PAUL

Our only freedom is to break the script.
Try it, be spontaneous!

JAKOB
(rolling eyes)

You don't get it! Even your newfound in-
sanity is predetermined! Think about it,
now that you have knowledge of the inescap-
ability of things, your mind acts out, just
like a spring uncoiling once its resistance
is lifted. It's basic physics. Nothing can
be changed, it's all part of the original
pattern.

PAUL
(suddenly looking somber, looking to the
distance)

You're absolutely right.

JAKOB
(in a serious tone)

Our submission or resistance to the inevitable is already part of the universal
script. There is no escape, no matter what
we do...

PAUL
(plants his face into both palms)

We're pawns.

                    JAKOB

We're puppets.

                    PAUL

Cogs in the wheel.

                    JAKOB

Automata.

(Both sigh simultaneously. After 30
seconds of silence, they look up at the
screen).

                    JAKOB

That was a beautiful goal, wasn't it?

                    PAUL

A stroke of genius.

                    JAKOB

Never again will we see another like
him.

PAUL

An immortal legend.

JAKOB

Simply the Greatest of All Time.

(After a period of silence, PAUL yawns
while JAKOB scratches his head).

JAKOB

The female national handball team is
coming up next.

PAUL

I don't mind staying for another round.

JAKOB

Two beers coming up.

(JAKOB walks up to the end of the stage
while PAUL attempts to make some random
movements in the air with his arms. After a
split second, he sighs and rests his chin
on his right hand. JAKOB returns with two
pints of beer.)

                    PAUL

Thanks mate, always a pleasure to hang
with my partner in crime.

                    JAKOB

    The pleasure is always mine. Cheers!

    (They lift their glasses for a toast.)

                    PAUL
            (in genuine satisfaction)

To whatever must come.

                    JAKOB

    To what shall be!

                    PAUL

To the pattern!

                    JAKOB

    To the fractal!

PAUL

To our next rejected screenplay!

JAKOB

To irremediable failure!

(Both men attempt to smile while bring-
ing their glasses to their mouths. JAKOB
drinks the entire glass in one gulp, PAUL
barely tastes his).

PAUL

I got one question though . . .

JAKOB
(waving his hand, watching the screen)

Shhh… the game is about to start…

SLOW CURTAIN

THE END

It is the nature of the human mind to change opinions much like a weathervane. Last night, after finishing that short one-act play, I felt I had finally broken a barrier. I had harnessed my feral pen, allowing only measured sentences (in dialogue form!) to carry a weak, but not completely unsatisfying, narrative. Today, after my croissants and—I'm also holding myself back on food—only two spoonsful of Nutella, I was afflicted with the worst case of acid reflux after rereading what I wrote last night. These characters are not credible, their expressions are too contrived, the development is too hasty, the finale underwhelming. I must start again from a remote corner of the literary map. Don't go for modes of fiction that have already been mastered. It's time to invent a new style, my own private paroxysm of language, a tiny aberrance of metaphor not yet labeled or defined.

> *Keep playing your silly role of dandy intellectual,*
> *make sure you keep writing, experimenting, publishing,*
> *whatever it takes to remain relevant in the market*

You know you are going to die. Regardless of your beliefs, this incarnate earthly existence must come to an end. You are just living mindlessly, jumping from one task to the next, colliding with events as they come rushing toward you, without a single moment to clearly see the panorama. When will you pause and step out of the hamster wheel? Drop your responsibilities, all pretense, become empty of purpose, lose sight of the future to catch your first, fully expansive, minute? What is this that you are certain you will lose? This piece of toast slathered in Nutella; come closer to its sponge-like surface, like some rectangular beach with heaps of crunchy mounds of dried sand. How does the last piece of toast on earth taste like? What alchemical decoction of crop, kneading, heat sublimates into this smell? Take a long breath and in this aroma become isolated from the space where things happen, and meaning is labored. Stay with me here, looking at the way the coffee cup holds its shadow like a dark aura. The stillness of objects as they wait to be used. The quiet indifference of being un-noticed. An inanimate object's ongoing surrender to lack of change. You are still in that timeless minute. No longer sub-mitting to the urge for action. Observing, *sub specie aeternita-tis*, the debris time left on your desk. A single strand of hair, crumbs from half-eaten toast, smudges of Nutella, the muti-lated column of a chewed pencil, the fissures on the wooden surface, the calm insistence of the lamp's light on the dust-cov-ered Canon A-1 camera. Your breath, the memory of inhaling a second ago. Time, an elaborate illusion motored by memory. Every arising moment moves like frozen vapor. In this intense intimacy with time, where every moment is an excruciating birth emerging from stillness, can you do anything except con-template the spectacle that keeps on vanishing? This temporal river is carrying everything into an obscure delta in the future. Can you break free from the stream of time by absorbing—like air into your lungs—the momentum of decay? To exit time by immersing yourself in this constant universal flux, to lose sight of your bodily boundaries long before the light of your awareness is extinguished by the unforgiving waters of change. Learn to die before you die.

Perhaps there are readers out there that are not looking for linear narratives, people who have begun to see life, like literature, as a collection of disjointed impressions, situations and circumstances that constantly shift positions; one day you are the top of the world, the next moment you feel abandoned in the haze of uncertainty, one moment you are in the company of the most enchanting people, the next moment you are a thin diffused shadow crawling through the prickly surface of solitude. A juxtaposition of extremes with long intervals of monotonous superficiality. Such people don't need a pretty story with a beginning and an end; convoluted though it may be, they expect nothing but a strange combination of short, impermanent snippets serving as an extension and expression of the eerie flux of life itself.

lies that allow ungifted individuals like you
to appear as literary pioneers

The teeth of the world are at my gate. My reaction as prey is to stare, immobile, quiet as a patch of moss. The world does not know it is a world. It is not conscious of my awareness that it is a predator waiting for my slightest blunder. Look at those jaws, translucent, shimmering as blades of light. The world's hunger has been stalking me since I first opened my bleary eyes—that original shaft of light scarring my newborn mind. The primordial fang, the blazing edge of trauma forever etching the course of my behavior. What we see in the arena of light will necessarily be the source of our understanding of change, objects will break, plants will grow, toys will be worn, parents will age and pass away; once the category of change is well implanted in the mind, we will recognize that inevitable force everywhere, even in the intimacy of our thoughts, emotions, memories, and beliefs. Light will always be our pyrite treasure, impinging on us the delicacy of the visual world, while simultaneously revealing the natural course for all living creatures: their surrender to the appetite of death. World = Death. The world is the living embodiment of what death does. Ouroboros. The world is a cannibal—not even that—it practices autosarcophagy, it's addicted to consuming itself. The teeth of the world are at my gate but wait! I am as much of the world as is light and change. If the world has a mouth, I am its tongue. It will devour its own ability to communicate its destructive desire, oblivion will feast on oblivion, the abyss can only be filled with the world, the world can only liquify itself to drown in its own creation. I remain still like a mouse not out of fear, but because I am waiting for my queue to jump, awaiting the signal from my own hunger for dying, so I can finally leap into the quelling throat of the universe.

What is this need to keep poeticizing every thought that comes into my mind? The previous paragraph could have been four sentences long. Keep it simple: I was afraid of dying yesterday. The world looks intimidating. I have existential vertigo. There are days I wish for my own death. That'd be a better portrayal of what I was experiencing, but I can't even place my reflections within a real living context. No events take place except liminal episodes only I can relate to. It's too subjective to be intelligible. I'm not making an effort to be understood. All these abstruse cypselae roaming in weightless images, with nothing to attach to, only the abstract filaments of language traveling in the currents of the Poetic. Is that even English?

I'm ok with being a failure. How many human beings have failed in the course of history? Even as a rhetorical question, only a deep sense of modesty can be an acceptable response. So, why not walk proudly as another specimen of failure? Yes, I can't write anything agreeable. Whoever finds these notes will probably label this chunter as the delusional writings of a morose mind. But I am at ease, working through the haze of my thinking, sketching on paper all the shapes the mist makes as it transits through the empty fields of meaning. I should just double down on my lack of talent and write fluent incoherence. I know what this is. Should be titled A LABYRINTHINE SNAIL HOUSE.

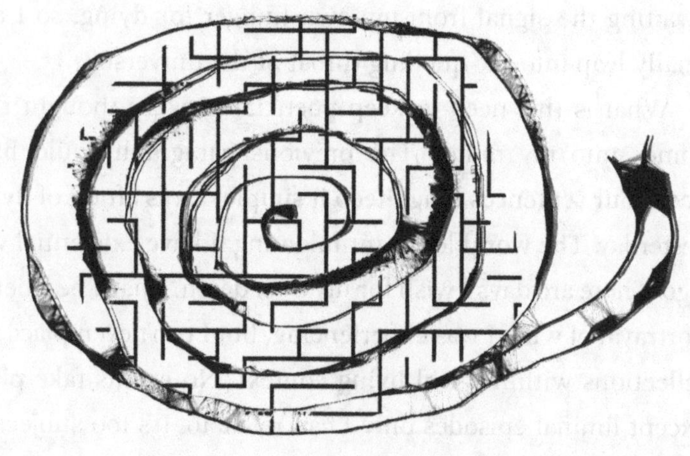

Too convoluted. The Snail House Maze: a rambling philosophical diary. Better.

Love. The topic that could sell millions of copies. Love and murder. People can't get enough of that stuff. The concept of love has always intimidated me. Those first few relationships with women, when a girl says *I love you* and you look blankly into her face, searching your whole spectrum of emotions, trying to identify that singular feeling that can be the unmistakable foundation for your reply: *I love you too*. I'm not sure I've been able to love in the way people so convincingly do. I can't untie love from all the other more palpable emotions: desire, fear, lust, apprehension, vulnerability. At some point, the mixture is so strong that I can look another person in the eye and calmly, but never surely, say: I love you. The intensity of the cocktail of emotions behind that sentence is the only proof I have that I actually love someone. But what makes it indubitable, as solid as a slab of granite? What sincerity linking mind and heart, what bridge between emotion and language, what transparency between past and present must there be, so the word love becomes a natural extension of the *love* you claim to... possess, fall prey to, embody, contain? So much of our lives hinges on this four-letter nounverb that it surprises me philosophers have not spent most of their lives trying to clarify this concept. Thales could have just as well started with: *Love is the strongest of things, for it rules everything.* A whole school of philosophy would have been built on that aphorism. But then again, it would have been the work of savants to show that love is not obvious at all, it is a confused concept, a misinterpreted emotion, a defective command; for we cannot chose when to love, when to feel it or, in any way, unanimously define it. It does not rule anything, it simply compels us to the most extreme actions; under the banner of love, war can be fought, suicide can be meaningful, death a respite.

I do not doubt my love for my son, a love that nonetheless fluctuates: It is diluted by tantrums of exasperation when I'm fatigued and overworked, enhanced if I haven't seen him in days while he's been with his mother, nurtured when the little brat spontaneously shows some affection, cooled when I'm in the zone, writing about existence as the shallow laughter of an inconsequential joke, redeemed when I look at his angelic face when he sleeps next to me, last thing I do every night when he's with me. Love is not a metaphysical root connecting us to the center of the cosmos, it is rather like a weak and fragile limb, a brittle twig peeking into the sky unaware that the dome is darkening as the first draughts of an approaching windstorm sway it.

    Are
        you
            essential
                in this
                    island
                of thought?
                      Or
                are
            you
              just
       another
      grain

of
fiction
in   the
stream   of   noise?

Many moments quiver like leaves at the end of frail limbs. You'll notice it when time is no longer insubstantial but begins to take form, a shape, almost object-like, as corporeal as ferns and stamens. Time, not the invisible stream on which events float, but as the blocks of materiality with which the arena of events is composed. Look at that singular minute, all nonuniform but smooth like obsidian! Right next to it is a decade, with its decadent façade, crumbling to pieces that accumulate as small pyramids of dust on the sturdy floor of a millennium. The seconds make curls of wind, with each instant traversing the air, small specks in mosaic configurations that are as graceful as they are unpredictable. The boulder of a million-year period scratches the sky, which is nothing more than the skin of one of the known eternities. Press your eye against the hole of tomorrow because look, yesterday's first hour is publicly mating with the most coveted year of this century. The afternoon is hyperventilating, after seeing the morning drop her robe. The sound of a leap year resonates like a

Is the world any richer for that lurid lunacy? I should have the courage to start deleting most of this melodious trash. It lacks credibility, context, commitment. I need to simplify things. Start with a banana. Observe it until you have memorized its shape. Feel its cool thick skin. Begin to undress it very slowly, noticing the very slight resistance of the ridges as you break the peel. Approach the soft white flesh and inhale its unmistakable aroma. Slightly press it against your cheeks, feel the faint smudge of starch left on your cheek bones. Then bring it closer after you have been detainingly studying it. It is time to bring it to your mouth. Part the lips; moisten them to reduce the friction as the elongated shaft makes contact with your tongue. Savor the rawness of the banana for a few seconds and then… bite the tip off! There, that's how I need to treat my literary subjects: build them without haste, properly consider the subject matter, come in close contact with them, chew them for a while before my prose spins out of control and, without any warranted poetic license, begins to decimate decades into dust.

Language hardly has the power to transcend the world it emerged from. Woodlice will only bear woodlice. It does not matter how radically you churn the substance of the world, there are always relationships you must respect. Agents performing actions, movement affecting objects, appearances dressed as images, thoughts structuring meaning, language dictating the pace and possibility of what is experienced. There can be no Copernican Revolution when it comes to language. You can spend the better part of four decades trying to understand how the mind fashions reality only to scribble down a brick volume of how you deducted—read: believe—time and space are innate aspects of cognition rather than attributes of external reality. Poor Kant. Any 21st century reader will be intimidated by his work, but in the end, it is just words on paper, thoughts imprisoned by the structure of grammar and syntax, ideas born from a world you could never transcend.

We believe that machines will one day evolve language to higher complexities, but even that faith is misplaced. Though novel technologies can create texts that, to all appearances, are cogent and insightful, people are missing the special ingredient that gives all this technological prowess its power. Namely, the meaning of the language being created must be interpreted by a mind, and at this point in time, the only consciousness capable of interpreting the significance of words is our own feeble awareness. Even if machines will one day create masterpiece after masterpiece, the validation of those works must happen *within* us, we must be able to render the text into human understanding; the capacity for a machine to impress us will ultimately depend on our own innate ability to manufacture meaning inside our brains.

I've done experiments in the past, attempting to portray the highly charged psychotic state of mind that a future civilization might one day harbor. I dream one day of rendering language as unpredictable and random as particles in Brownian motion, while preserving its inexhaustible proneness to dress reality with thin images. The closest I have come to this was an opera in three voices, written for the inveterate mystics of the future.

Before the performance begins a presenter stands in the middle of the stage to make this announcement:

This is not a performance to be understood, this is a mystery to be experienced. There

are no characters in this story. The voices
are both real and imaginary. You are both
spectator and protagonist. Allow the words
to flow through you the same way water flows
through your fingers. Swim in the music as if
it were a vast metaphysical sea. Remember:
you are giving this all the meaning it has.

Lights out. Lights on. Lights out. Music
begins. We hear:

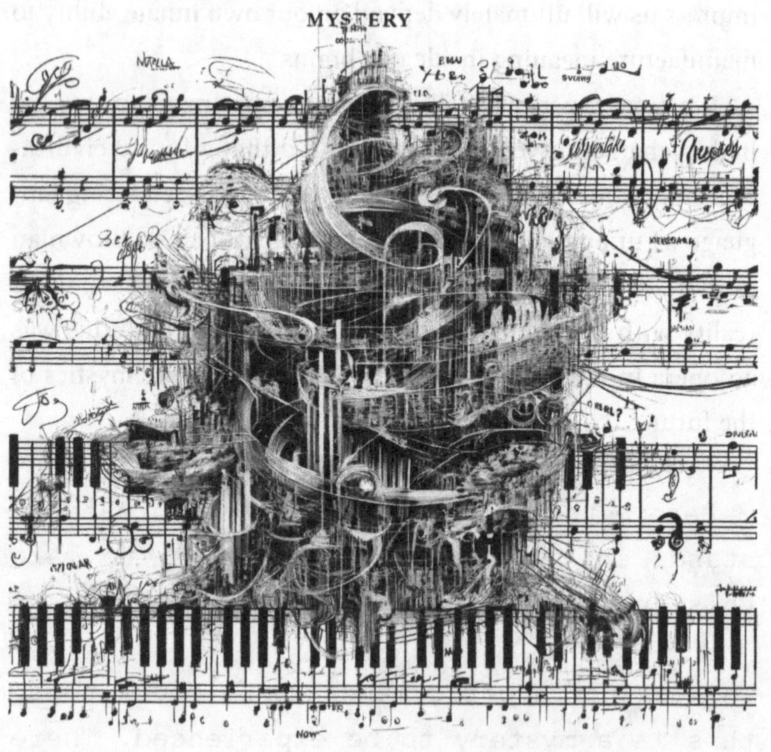

You're made of blue music
the inevitability of sadness.

Voice #1:
[Introvert, as if thinking out loud, hand
to forehead]
I am not alone weaving the sound of my
new name.
What is this mist now
an infant thing
meaning is violent
my voice is a great fire.

The flame spells my name and purity shines
in the first morning

[All three voices, harmonic:]

of smoke

[All 3 performers, sitting crossed-
legged:]

I invented the great sun

Voice #2:
Pre-Object

Voice #3:
Post-Logical

Voice #1:
Do not merge with another story; I am the… a… of a deep crevice.
Mystery is the very meaning of the question. This is me, a flame without a name.

Voice #3:
Origin everywhere.
Nothing to shelter me…
I am … the *here* that all places share.

[Dark stage. Low trembling sounds from orchestra, the inner tension before a world comes into being. Pulsating sounds gather strength until there is a moment of silence.]

Look at the weight of its horror.
When's perception? But as the space for every moment to brandish a heart.

V#3:
Do you hear that piece of sky over there?
Long awful avenues of world, great thick universe!

V#2:
The Part is more actual than the Whole.
There is no world. Inside the ocean of
life, there is nothing to fear.

[backdrop video off]

A creature crawls over there in the dis-
tance…[pause] I am that creature.
Desert as far as the eye can see.
Speech bloated with black & blue wonders.

V#3 [furthest back, as scanning both audience and other two performers]:

What was the sound light made as it crashed
against the first piece of world?
From absolute change, I now crawl between
the farts of chaos.

V#1:
This emptiness round as an orgasm. I am
standing below my own ecstasy.

[low, confessional tone toward the audi-
ence]

[Faster movement of lights, slightly in-
tensified]

To allow meaning to exit
the earth?

V#2:
Wreckage. Mounds of Language. I am here.
[opens eyes]
I saw a cloud, I have seen angels bathe
[hopeless, at the verge of total resigna-
tion, perhaps on his knees]
inside an echo.

V#2:
Matador!
Cloaked   as   Voice   #1   [3rd
light   turns   on   above   performer]:
Nothing really ever happens. At all.

------ Scene 2 ------

----- end of scene ----

V#2:
Actors or agents, ignore all my useless passion.

V#3: [higher pitched, wondering]
Nondescript sound.
[as performer speaks this line, first stable but then subtle light appears from above the performer]

V#1 [Confident, equanimous]:
To have felt the sharp rivers aching,
in the beginning darkness flowed uninhibitedly.

------ Scene 1 reimagined ------

3 Voices in unison:
Deluge of darkness.
Desert supporting the night sky with the bricks of silence.
Whatever travels in echo, the echo breaks free from its shell, the echo eclipses its music.
You see, I own a camel that drinks from a pool of darkness.
I am here in the shape of all meaning.

V#1:

This thirst for truth, this hunger for symbols.

Voice X [any actor can step in here, including you]:

[gesturing with hands the flow of water and then pointed to its head]

But now we are lost in the storm of dreaming.

[electronic sounds, with recurring pulsating beat until we reach a moment of sudden silence]

V#3:

There will be many errors in this performance. Flaws that will be revealed as flaws. A work that is aware of its own weakness. Whoever conceived this must not be human, not animate. This is more like the behavior of light, something so light it evaporates as rising mist.

----- Scene 3 -------
V#1: [dispersed motions, exploring the emptiness of the stage]
Symbols still too wide to be meaningful.

Still inside the walls of a glowing dream.
[confused awakening, in which they ex-
plore their empty surroundings - the stage
- as if witnessing the *mysterium tremendum*
itself.]
I am …
[as next line is spoken, brighter powerful imagery, accompanied by powerful surge
of music]

V#3:
Carrying the paradox of pain.
Myself? As spherical as an egg.

[Video: cloud formations and lightning
in slow motion. Example: www.theparadoxof-
painandthejoyofsuffering.com]

V#1:
[blissful]
Everything rests again,
[coming closer to audience]
there are no boundaries to your center.
You are not inside the world but around
it.
Watch:

V#2:
This is are was will can must be shape-
less.

V#3:
You Seeker!

V#2:
You Particle!

V#1:
Soon we will dance and feast on phenomena.

Voice #1 and #2:
I saw the darkness. "self-reference to
this body"

V#3:
Liminality: this civilization owns more
dark than gold.

V#1:
Long ago I was often mistaken for the
sound coiled inside the invisibility of
meaning.

But I brought fire into the night, to melt
the gloom.

[Video: glimpses of night sky footage,
Milky Way… the Milky fucking Way]

V#3:

Let it be spoken. Where's experience? I
am order gaining in strength. I would cut a
star-shaped hole in the fabric of thought.

V#2:

Genitals hard against the enigma.
To & for silence.

V#1:

How is my body a particle in love with
vibration?

[closes eyes again]

[video off]

V#2:

I found emptiness, this vastness will
force us to make infinite analysis.

V#3:

Lips sucking on shadows, a perfect crater. Of music.

V#1:

[points to the distance off stage]
I am …
I was before my name melted back into the
wind.

[Time lapse of an animal being 'eaten' by
ants. Example: Use your own imagination.]

V#2:
This structure to the dream will explode,
in a liquid, trembling mind.

V#3:
Inside the very smell of galaxies.
All these faces waiting for me to trans-
form into wings.

Listen to the voice of audience not knowing
they are audience.

[video on, but very thin imagery]

V#2:
Oblivion.
Darkness again.
Pure light without sight.
There are no walls to this earth,
[hushing motion, finger to lips]
like tombstones arched around the
the substance of chance.

V#3: [very airy movements, light, careless as ether]

From the soil of silence, a pulse of life
escaped.
Knowledge now eats parts of itself.

----- end of scene ----

----- Epilogue ----

V#1:
Time has lost its river. Memory:
a shell of ash around a pale fire.

V#1 (again):
Laughter
Earth, solid as stone.
Laughter again. [Audience laughs]

V#1 (once again):
Metaphor
[pointing to its head and then using hands
to simulate a machine in operation]
Hush.
Was I once what the wind erodes into silence?
I am still inside mind-etched hell, still
inside the womb of madness. I borrow language as a perfume, the rest is silence.

V#3: [hopeful, eager]

This is not a story.
What blind history drops us into this mess?
There are no beginnings or endings,
I have enough room to absorb the abyss.

V#3:
Nothing but song lasts.
A great fire, pale blue eternally unspoken... all knowledge is ash.

I never finished it. How could I? What's the logic in it... Works well when you are at the end of your ropes, ready to abandon the putative alliance between world and language. Music alleviates the sensation of asphyxiation, it massages Wernicke's area as you surrender to meaning that cannot be immediately grasped, only intuited as glimpses of the primordial chaos, where symbols wrested themselves out of the immensity of silence. *Life is not a problem to be solved but a reality to be experienced.* Plagiarizing again. Only this time I don't know who I'm stealing from. People attribute a similar quote to Nietzsche, Kierkegaard, Frank Herbert, Alan Watts, and J. J. van der Leeuw, just to mention those I'm aware of. Making it clear everyone takes from everyone else; the origin of meaning as obscure as the mystery we're trying to decipher.

For months, the sun has not come out. The wind and rain are one single entity, smothering the world in one continuous sensation. The world as idea. No, the world as perception. The blades of grass, gracefully bending under the voice of the wind. Droplets roll down the windowpanes as streaks of the world's sadness. No, the world is not my perception. I'm in the perception of the world. The clouds are unanimously agreeing to mutate into the wildest expressions of phantasmagoria. The mirror, for all its fidelity, is only the slice of a shining dream, giving me the impression that I am here. I am that I am. The ultimate syllogism, one that only a god can speak. Am I certain that I am? Look at the lens of the camera, blind when no one presses on the shutter. What am I without a piece of the world somehow becoming aware, able to notice that I am, a body, an organism, a human being? Who would I be without memory's ability to keep a loose chronological tab of events? What would I become if thoughts did not coalesce into bubbles of meaning—if the dualistic tendency of language hadn't marked the boundary of where I end, and the universe begins? What is life if not an overwhelming blot of sensation?

I've noticed a bulge on my left foot. Worrying. It gets red at times, itches, heaves. A pedestrian lung. Are my nightly hallucinations real occurrences? Get real, I can't lose touch of reality that easily. I know what it is. A tumor. Cancerous growth. No, an unknown disease. A freak abnormality that affects one in every two hundred million people. An incurable illness, the first symptom of a long chain of ailments that will hail the end. I knew it would happen, sooner or later. An accident, a heart attack, an irreversible sickness. I'm ready for it. What could I change, the Rubicon has been crossed. These are the last shadows to brush past the arc of my eyes. The mutiny of my own cells will conquer my will to live. These are the last days of action. How can I make the best of it? Is it time for me to step it up and write like there is nothing more to lose? The vanity of the anthropocentric view. The world will continue with or without us. Regardless of what I leave behind, everything will be consumed in loops of infinite change. Even these texts are just like any other daily act consigned to oblivion.

My gosh, listen to that. I'm like tape, layer after layer of cliché. Sentimental bullshit… consigned to oblivion. What can even impress the cynical hearts of the 21st century? People are immune to awe. All the superficial Wows, Awesomes, Blew-my-minds. If I could give them something they've never experienced before, something of the magnitude of a super being—an irrefutable, unquestionable, definitive encounter with a godlike appearance. The encounter must be in the innermost region of the mind. The external world goes blank. A block of eternal possibility squarely in the center of your awareness. A door you can walk through, a room you can enter. The air is pure intelligence. The second you breathe in the elegance of this unending intellect; your awareness of the inner world vanishes as well. But there is no nothingness. There is an awake existence creating itself. You feel identical to every act that comes forth. You are creating the world *ex nihilo*. Every curl of matter you move feels like blood rushing through your veins. Every instant is a spark you have kindled. This is absolute freedom; the arena of the universe is being invented by your seeing it. There is no inside or outside. There is just pure becoming, with every bit of it awake, pregnant with untiring potential—you are the Godhead behind all that happens. Your body is the body of the world. Your heartbeat is the pulse that enacts time. You are the center of everything that has been, is and will ever be. You can become an insect, mycelium, black matter, a human being, a speck of dust consuming an eternity while floating around a candle. There are no limitations to what you can become awake to. To perceive is to be, the Bishop was right. You have always been one step ahead of evolution. Blink and the world will shift shape. Close your eyes and you'll enter a void of a thousand years.

How can I nail my thoughts to the flesh of experience? Nothing I say clings to the world. I take it too far, far too quicky. How can I dress actual experience with the coat of my abstract poetics? There are many, much more profound writers out there that tell a story, and with the images of the story, fashion a deep and resounding philosophy. Palpable wisdom, incarnated insights that transform the way we see the world. I pick up an interesting thought and immediately fling it into intercosmic space. Can't keep more than a few sentences hovering above the ground; there is this pathetic compulsion to transcend our petty world. I would be of better use to the world if I carved out rocks. A stone sculptor. At least I'd leave something behind that could be felt with the hands, an object that could be walked around, a surface that could cast an actual shadow. Half-born gnomes, stunted monsters that will never emerge from their father's basement. Their creator constantly hesitating, changing style mid-work, experimenting without settling into his own style, an underachiever of epic proportions, incapable of attaining a fully-fledged artform. If only I had the consistency to leave an army of aberrant stumps in a basement. My own Terracotta Army of failure.

An ability for storytelling is not like a muscle that you must train, it's more like a necessity you succumb to. I can imagine writers of real caliber running endless scenarios in their minds that they can't wait to pen down. I am, on the other hand, drifting in countless unfinished reflections about the world, language, doomsday, emptiness; always revolving around the futility of meaning and the absurdity of thought. I'm picking holes in the fabric of truth simply to justify my lack of determination in constructing a sensible theory. Contradictions abound in my writings. I despise the self-centeredness of our species and nonetheless I spend so much of my time analyzing my inability as a writer. The Catch-22 of Self-Deception. I see my own inconsistencies, the broad crater my lies leave on the surface of my thoughts. I pretend to not feel anything, to be above the pointlessness of trying or not trying. I profess to have "stopped playing the game" but there is this urgency to return every night to a piece of paper. Why do I keep taking notes in the back of books, which I supposedly don't read anymore? Look at the way language manipulates reality. I can make any claim, at any moment. Anything can be said about the world, anything! With a little charm, your fantasies can become veritable beliefs that propel your life.

It is so dull to keep writing about language itself. Obviously, it is a subject that fascinates writers. But some authors can build the ideas into stories, make fiction out of philosophy. Iris Murdoch did it brilliantly with *Under the Net*. I could taste my own bile when reading *Nausea*. If our absurd fate has ever been compressed into a novel, *The Stranger* is it.

I suspect that I will estrange any reader if I subject them only to the angry waves of my ideas, this whirlpool of delirium, without providing them with a raft, or at least a life preserver, so they can contemplate this mad sea of intellection without gasping in despair for air. I must find ways I can connect with other human beings. What could it be? Details of my life, my friends, my son, my aging mother, my lost loves, my rarely visited literary friends, my late father.

Fragments of an autobiography, part I

My son's eyes are crystals, wide awake, translucent sepals open to the world. I never planned to be a parent. It happened as readily as Tuesday turns into Wednesday. Was it love, or just a necessity that kept me by his mother's side long enough for the gametic union to occur?

(Slow down. Keep it simple. Don't try to impress with hard-sought biological terms. Tame that compulsion to metaphorize!)

I did not love his mother. She made me laugh, though. We sure loved to party till late at night. She had that natural *joie de vivre* I had previously seen only in my deceased friend, but she had no predisposition to grasp life from any philosophical viewpoint. Life was as it was. Coffee at eleven in the morning. Watering the plants. A jog along the river (she, not me). Lovemaking in any room of the small flat we shared for some time in Berlin. She'd talk to anyone around: the neighbors, people at bus stops, gatekeepers at public parks. She somehow managed to be occupied every minute of her day, while I'd spend countless hours in the flat, reading books, pondering over an obscure existential trifle. She'd often find me wallowing in a newfound pit of despair, only to brush away any comment I'd make when she entered the room: "Let's go for a walk, the weather is so nice!" She could pull me away from my thoughts so easily. And I did succumb to her way; for a period, I didn't need to frame my life in some nucleoid of reason. I stopped worrying about how to make it in the world of "literature". We listened to jazz, funk, techno, it didn't really matter; we went to the theater, or hung out by the Admiralbrücke listening to troubadours, sat till evening in a random nook of Görlitzer Park; we were content, living mindlessly the passing blur of each moment.

A couple of years later, on any random day, the sky did something strange. A combination of colors I've never seen before, a fusion of sarcoline, celadon, aureolin, eburnean painted the sky, we walked hand in hand, like two somnambulists under that wealth of mellow tones. Then she said: "I want your child."

I was not thinking, or perhaps I was thinking too clearly, so I said: YES!

Defying all odds, she was pregnant by the end of the month, even though she was entering her forty-first year and had previously spent three years trying to conceive a child with a former partner.

Thomas Julio Vladimir was born on a rainy October day. He took her away from me, all the attention went to our son. Without her snapping me out of my brooding states, taking me out of the apartment, making me laugh with the silliest jokes, I lost my existential connection to her. By then my first book was about to be released and I was busy finishing my second. It was not long before we felt alienated from each other and decided to raise this T. J. separately.

How about authoring a book whose sole purpose is to summarize other books in one sentence? Hundreds of famous works laconically defined. That could be a worthy endeavor. If only I could recall a fourth of a story in any book. I forget them as easily as I struggle to create a story. Perhaps I need to throw myself back into life. Have experiences. Travel again. Get myself a lover. Join literary circles. Get a job on the docks. Or become a postal worker. Could develop a destructive addiction to opioids. Lose touch with reality and walk the city believing I'm a Mongolian emperor. Anything that can help me develop a style whose language feels as good as dope. Read a bit of Borges every hour for an entire year so I can build my own literary labyrinth of extravagant subtlety. Or become a motivational speaker. Give readers dopamine hits through empowering slogans. Inspire people to nourish a new attitude toward this chaotic 21st century. A rebel's self-help book: seven steps to becoming a content loser. The four universal principles to doubt everything. Or go back to poetry. Poems that are whales who are telepathically broadcasting the language of an alien civilization. Or simply become incomprehensible. Write the bottomless history of an instant.

The first minute after you smoke, in hostile sling, behind recesses, toward erogenous zones, within the camouflage of rocks, immune to the mirror of forests, blown like a ribbon of music, past the bedroom of fire, inside the image of the sky, taking off the sweater of form, pumping image into the milk of time, groaning, grain by grain of storm, flickering rocket, torn misprinted sea, hatching miracle, birthing data, you are rushed to a pre-Christian domain, metal and glass are gold, mountains are throbs in your wrists, flotsam in a simulation, a citizenship of nature, the smell of leaves burning, earthworms writhing in pain, pitiless axis of the drums, the beat stretches gravity, nodding jewels, dirty retinas, blonde paranoid sun, winter curling about a helmet, the char of plans, shouts sailing the whole of the Arabian sea, the not-end of the heart, rumors present in the hay, penises so perfect you whistle, propulsion shaking the earth, quay collecting skulls, rains over the regime, your eyes are polished, soft as morning, carefully tasting the arc of sound, burying reality with so much snow, the whiteness of perfection; you have smoked a key, a laser that sears your lips, you undress from the modern calamity of knowing, the ecstasy of danger covers your entire skin, magicians' stars in a pocket of dust, logic is a tiny shape you crush, god is a child you play with, a bit of mercy is a foolish request, nothing but more and more of yes, columns of eternal summary, but truer to mud, you can sit contentedly watching at a strange angle the song of emptiness, beauty never sleeps here, vomit in tracts of rainbows, you caress the haze of memory, golden figures talk from the edges, incandescent words walk without shoes along the bridge of illusion, where are you is a question that vanishes as soon as it arises, objects are reluctant to be grasped, every hair is a rose, the head is a place of assembly, where ancient saucers course in linear not so linear paths, mildew in a plate of paradise, hermetic pleasures bulging around the lips, cities of rapture in each eyelash, pathways miles long for wave after wave; you are eaten alive by hoarse ants, speed makes scars in the sound that approaches you, you are the whole thing, learning to be length in this spiraling captivity, meek of mouth you struggle to engineer a single statement, instead you are a spear ready to kiss the voice of creation, pure word newly created, gathering brightness, breather of darkness, motor blazing across the stations of silence, kill me you beg but the syllables are honey crystalizing around your tongue, the pure word builds its own body, your body thickens into a monolith, the past is a pillow, you are ready to sleep dream awake die, you are tightening every muscle to hear the purest of words, mountains stare at your wonder, the behavior of the journey cradles you in half a hemisphere, the diamond of language truth reality is finally within arm's reach, from this stone you will build your own church, drool tears sweat squeezing out of you, light wavers like an infinite ocean, sibilant clouds announce the moment, it is here, packed in number, thawing as an immense glacier, despair sickness death cannot detain you, you are about to be revealed the only nugget of being that matters, your eyes are diaphanous windows, your ears are cathedrals of prayer, in front of you the Realest of the Real, the meaning around which creation orbits, the colossal fetus of totality opens its wings, nothing but this, it is being spoken, the shape of its power is being set free, you are ready: it speaks…. Hey, how was the ride?

When I awoke from the "trip", my friend was sitting placidly by my side. Hey, how was the ride? I looked at him dumbfounded. I was so close to seeing the Everything in everything, the All in all. Just before the final revelation was made, I came back to this world. I shrieked: Let me back in! but it was too late. Mundane reality had again settled in, and I was on the floor sweating with my friend's benevolent smile just above my face. I had been reading the Doors of Perception for the third time and decided it was time for me to finally transcend my self-limitations. My friend, who I hadn't seen in a couple of years, had been working with medicinal plants and extremely powerful drugs in an old countryside home about an hour and a half away from where I live. I told him I could not do one of those substances that would leave me tripping for twelve hours, so he suggested I smoke a bit of one of the most potent psychedelic chemicals known to humans. The "trip" would take only ten to twenty minutes but would feel like a lifetime.

A compressed eternity it was indeed. Intense streams of data flowing through my mind. It almost felt as if I'd been blind all my life and suddenly was allowed to get a glimpse of the spectrum of light. But the experience has faded, my recollections of the visions or "events" during my journey are now vague and somewhat disfigured by this need to translate them into language. I did get an inkling of what I've been writing about in the past. In fact, I was a bit spooked by the uncanniness of the experience vis-à-vis the text I wrote only a week ago about our cynical 21st century hearts. As convincing as the experience was, the question now remains whether there is any lasting reward from this "hyperdimensional" encounter, other than the sensation that no matter what metaphysical stunts we might undertake, the farthest we can travel is up to the edge of the abyss, where we stare in dumb silence at the nondescript vast emptiness, immobilized by the *mysterium tremendum* of the beyond, only to turn around and return to our homes to slouch in a sofa and eat a bar of chocolate.

"As you get older, the meaning of what you see will change, *hijo*. The river of life will take you with it, even if you resist its currents. Son, look at these hands. They are like the skin of an elephant. They used to be smooth, full of life. Now they hurt when I press on the maize dough. The meaning of life can be found in this lump of dough. It's malleable and conforms to the shape you want to give it. When you are young, you have ideas of what is important. These ideas will get flattened, as I am doing now with the dough. They will have a definite shape and be fried into the roundness of a tortilla. The shape can't be changed now, you're stuck with this form. What I'm trying to say is that the endless possibilities of youth are reduced to fixed patterns. When you get older you will appreciate the flatness of the tortilla more than the freedom of giving any shape to the dough. Live contentedly with your fate, don't tempt it. Don't ask for too much or you will fall into the traps of the devil. You know I have always been a believer, even though I don't go to church anymore. I believe the invisible world is more powerful than the world we can touch. Don't roll your eyes. Trust your old mother. Please pray to your patron saint. He will guide you through tough times, give you the strength to swallow the burnt, bitter edges of the tortillas life will serve you. The day will come when there will be no more tortillas on the kitchen table. When you reach my age, a crumb is worth more than basket full of *cajetas*. Have you noticed how the daily ration of tortillas doesn't last as it used to? Time speeds up as you age, but there is always room to slow down and look at the beautiful details around you. I have stared at the smoke from the hearth for years and never get bored. Sometimes I get a deep sense of mystery and awe just by looking at normal things. *Objetos* we overlook too easily. I often feel the presence of God when I look at the smoke. I know you don't believe in Him. But at least feel the wonder of His creation. Pay close attention to the details around you. There is more meaning in that than in all your aspirations put together. I am getting closer to leaving this world. It's a world of pain and struggle, but I'm grateful to have been put here. To see, despite the suffering, the delicate beauty of things. Plants. Clouds. The sea. Go to the sea often. The sight of the water will heal your hurts. Touch the sand. It is like touching the hands of the Creator.

I know you laugh inside when I talk like this. The world is changing, I get it. Young people don't believe in anything anymore. I have accepted that too. But just because my world is not yours, don't assume that everything I say is unreasonable. Take a break from your understanding. Listen with your innermost sense. You will discover something divine inside nature. Don't call it God, I don't care. But get a taste of that ever-present fountain. If only once. You can make up any story later about what it is and what it means. I can tell you how it feels to me. I become a child again, even at my age, when I get lost in the reverie of contemplating this smoke, I feel like I never have seen smoke before. It is miraculous. The way it moves, gets entangled in itself and then vanishes into thin air. My heart gets overwhelmed, I cry and thank the Lord for giving me the gift of seeing His creation as it is. Eat a tortilla, they are freshly made. Yes, they are very soft. Smell them, the harvest this year has been great. The maize is so juicy. Mmhmm, it is a special year. Your father passed away a year ago. I thought I would die within a year after his death. I felt so lonely, lost in the fog of my thoughts. The Lord helped me through this difficult period. Faith is like a boat. It can carry you. Don't laugh. You are a smart boy. You are good with words. *El juego del lenguaje.* You explained that to me long ago. You can just change the words I use to fit your view. Don't call it Faith. Call it something else, whatever grants you the strength to confront each day. Call it *Mystery* or the *Enigma.* I know you like *palabrillas* like those. You are old enough to know time is a strong current. Look at my *nieto.* He's growing so fast lately. Are you spending enough time with him? Put your life aside for those early years. Every day is a treasure. Soon he will have grown up and made a life of his own. The life of work and worry. Learn from him while he is still a child. Relearn the ability to play. Observe how he dances, jumps, spins, rests, the way he looks at things. We forget how easy it can be. You'll be made new from spending time with a child. Take another tortilla before they get cold. I'm going to hang the laundry soon. Stay if you want. Take a nap. I have some *leche condensada* if you want to dip your tortilla in it. It is nice seeing you, *hijo*. Remember to smile more often. I don't like seeing you so glum. The river of life will take you places, into regions of the heart you didn't know you had, if you allow it to. Relax a bit and learn to float. Have Fai... trust the power that is pushing the current. Nature. The *Mystery*, *hijo*. The *Mystery*."

My mother used to embarrass me when she spoke about religion in my younger years. Her *lenguaje* doesn't seem so bizarre now. I am starting to see each person as a little prickly tip that pokes the tiniest hole in the fabric of the unknown. Each person gets to see only the smallest bit of the *Mystery*. Each person will, within the bounds of their available vocabulary and texture of their thought, describe to the best of their ability what they see and, as is inevitable with humans, prescribe a certain behavior or attitude toward the *Great Enigma*.

Language is like an empty vessel which we fill with the contents of our subjectivity. Give free rein to language and it can invent anything, giving reality whatever shape the mind is capable of conceiving.

I can already hear the stalwarts of morality: this is absolute relativism. If there is no sound ground to the meaning we possess, anarchy will ensue. Any mad person can come and whip up an ideology that can wipe us off the map. To which I respond: don't be ridiculous, language has always been malleable as a piece of playdough. It is supple and eager to assume the shape we give it. But don't despair. What you fear might happen has already been happening to some degree. Corrupted minds will project a corrupted world. It matters little if we today become consciously aware of the relativity of language. That won't accelerate our path toward extinction. You see, language follows its own logic, there are riverbeds through which language must flow; it is naïve to assume we can just create any worldview out of nothing. The mind is only capable of building from the level from which it arose. It is embedded in rules of thought, modes of morality, concepts of justice, regardless of how vehemently we may suppress or deny these notions. And why even take my words so seriously, I can't control much of what I write anyway. These ideas arise on their own inside my head. I can only slightly modulate the narrative that is streaming through, a deeper necessity is at play here; some imperceptible but grand factory of meaning is behind the world we know. My words, in any case, don't carry any absolute meaning. In the long run they might even galvanize people's innate desire to defend and further fortify humankind's most cherished belief: that with good intentions, we may bring good to the world.

Change feels good. Seeing my mother, experimenting again with mind-altering substances. I'm even writing sometimes in the mornings now. Who knows, by early next year I'll have a new manuscript ready.

The sun has been out for a few days now. The dust can be clearly seen on the surface of things. I am able to discern the wild mutations the air makes above the radiator when it briefly paints its shadow-like swirls on my wooden desk. I have nothing more to say about this particular moment. The house is quiet. I don't seem to have the inclination to write or not to write. Read a book, maybe. Write a poem? Should I get back to writing poems, rather than these incongruous texts that will end in a waste basket someday?

Sun
out
few
days
now. The dust's.
    There. On
    The surface   of things.
I am
the wild mutations.
Nature composes.
The air likes me.
    Makes shadow-like swirls
    on the wooden desk.

Who paints the music of the air?
In this particular moment: The house is quiet.
Write   to   write or not to write to be here.

Empty your book, maybe.

Polish the surface of language. Make it a window.

Only the world is here.

Empty the poems of us.

The
sun
has
been
out
for a
an
endless
hour
now.

This narrow life. The circumference of everything we see is delineated by the roundness of the clock. The minute lines, like some ancient monolithic monument, the Stonehenge of temporality, is our golden cage. We are free to walk away from this unlocked enclosure, but we prefer to remain within the custody of the constant cycle.

The Circle

She read:

We've been sitting in a circle staring at stones undaunted by the unreachable aim that brought us here. This is long after meditation was supplanted by MetaVoice, a nature-tech that inspired our attempts at real transcendence. While MetaVoice can be proven in each of the thirty scientific paradigms currently contending to become the first to quantify and predict 0.01% of the known universe—thus to break Dual-Quanta's undisputed thousand-year record (a success that has faded since 0.0094% became a static embarrassment among its ninth generation and subsequent followers)—our approach hinges on the supposition that the meaning that emerges from our field of experience is no way apt to grasp the underlying ontology that reverberates as a faint echo in the reality we believe to be based in. MetaVoice is the emancipation of language from the mind; scientists have been able to accurately measure 'language streams' the same way ultraviolet or gamma rays can be recorded. The discovery of the independence of language as a cosmic phenomenon has accelerated the progress of science to such an extent that today we know how much we know and how much we lack in truth. It has likewise enriched long-standing spiritual traditions that now train their inner attention to the spikes and structures that arise in MetaVoice, rather than the sensations of their body. Our circle has assembled an ecology of self-doubting minds that thrive in the detection of paradoxes. From the understanding that understanding lives outside our minds the same way birds fly freely in the air away from their nests, our circle is now exploring a possible new nature-tech we call AntiHere. We are staring at stones that we know are not just only stones. We focus intensely on the language streams they emit (language is not exclusive to humans, even inanimate matter has its own syntax), listening to their rough rudimentary language as it escapes into the open air. We concentrate on the stone not being stone, on their language not being spoken, on the pause hidden between being and becoming. The stones, without seeing us, speak about us amongst themselves. They say our bodies are stones. That we are ancient dead chunks of the cosmos radiating thought. They watch time evaporate from our heads. The stones suddenly watch us watching them. Their blindness studying our own. We reassemble the science that is being invented in their language. We polish the mirror reality borrows to comprehend itself. We listen to the silence that coats MetaVoice. The stones keep sinking in their own void; we follow them into their abyss to deepen our ignorance. We lose ourselves in this infinitesimal nook of the universe. Sitting in a circle staring at stones, our humanity dissolves below the voice of time. Undaunted by the unreachable aim that brought us here, we continue our pursuit:

to touch the surface of death

to pull death's dreams from
the surface of the stones

to dream new scars
in the body of time

to make time bleed its language
over our naked bodies

to laugh with the stones
in their eternal silence.

When she finished reading the pamphlet there was no more doubt left in her mind. Her body advancing in a weightless gait. She had become transparent to the world. Fearless, an iota of uncrushable being. This is one of thousands of pamphlets circulating in the streets. People were waking up. Reality was not what it was taken to be. The greatest philosophers of the past had only been brushing away the prehistoric crust of dirt from the collar bone of a gigantic creature, whose dimensions, features, and behavior were beyond all the classifications we had employed so far. Existence was an outdated book, and it was about to be rewritten. She feels it in her marrow. She is going to change her name. From Lila to Omnia. Omnia Nihil. The nascent shape of a new reality. Not human, not earthbound. Dimensions are highways we will soon ride, each speck of being on its own adventure. Everyone will be their own spark of genius. There is more mystery in an ounce of time than in all the books written about life and death. The limitations of thought were thawing in her mind, like barricades of ice exposed to the flame of truth. The light of that fire spells the simple irrevocable fact: Your life is your own projection.

You set the rules of the game. You impris-
on yourself within the confines of your own
limiting beliefs. *The Circle* was just the
last knock needed to smash the bullshit of
her self-doubt. She was a block of infinite
possibility. There were other pamphlets doing just the same to other minds. There was
Demolishing the Edifice of Shame, *The Corridors of this Dream*, *An Analogy between
Trees & Minds*, *How the Ghost Escaped the
Rocket*, *Music is the Voice of Time*, *Mirrors
for the Echo of Light*, *Wake Up from Being
Dead*, etcetera. Whole legions of people were
coming to terms with the basic inescapable
principle: behind any meaning, there is the
faculty to apprehend the meaning. Stop lingering in the arena of meaning, step back
into the field of the witness that appre-
hends the meaning. There lies the treasure
of unbounded potential. Omnia Nihil was already beginning to feel her mind coexist-
ing at various places, refracting through
the prism of truth into the fable of past,
present and future. Omnia began hearing the
voices of other awakened beings. They could
speak through walls, across countries,
through the rampart of time. Her mind was
not her own, it was just a temporal vessel
to condense a particular pattern of person.

She has nothing and everything at the same
time. A hyperdimensional adventure was to
unfold.

    to pull death's dreams from
    the surface of the stones

    to dream new scars
    in the body of time

    to make time bleed its language
    over our naked bodies

    to laugh with the stones
    in their eternal silence.

THE BEGINNING

The end is always a beginning. An offshoot of all past actions and events. Unknown ramifications will unfold from the
tiniest cause. How a writer determines an ending is always an
arbitrary decision. The abandonment of fiction only for the
Real to take over. The text always survives to some degree in
the mind of the reader. Text is like a virus. A person innocently
reads a book but those new ideas, those novel language forms,
begin to take root and multiply within the person's brain. They
won't paralyze the mind. It is not a parasite that takes control. It is a love fest, each virus intermingling with the other

text viruses, engendering unique strings of language, initially sharpening the lens of the person's biases and predispositions, but, eventually, every now and then, there is a mutation. A person changes their mind, shifts their beliefs, abandons faith, or gains an ideology. Through an unknown mechanism the person becomes satiated with a previous thought system and moves on to a new terrain. There is a tipping point that remains unexplained. The moment an alcoholic commits to the path of their recovery. The instant a person loses faith to become an incorrigible atheist. The day I break free from my own philosophical chains and wander inside the unexamined life peacefully.

As you get closer to the end of a book you are reading, there is this innate desire to capture the story in its entirety, to admire the evolving interrelationships of the characters, the sharp turns of fate, the wondrous synchronicities the world enacts behind the protagonists' backs, the ingenuity of the writer who played with our expectations by masterfully revealing only crumbs of the pie. Then, when we take a fleeting bite of that tartlet, we close the book with what is often a dissatisfied sigh. Emptiness ensues. Ennui. The story is over, and life must resume. Without the extravagance of the twists and turns of a superb plot, without the liveliness of incomparable characters, without the advantage of performing a role scripted by a Master of Literature. The frustration of having been shown the potential of language, to have glimpsed the profusion of the human imagination, to have savored the scrumptious texture of human thinking, only to end in the tedium of looking at two flies copulating on the ceiling.

Ennui. What a wonderful word. Ambiguous. Absurd. Incomprehensible. Enigmatic. Ephemeral. Ineffable. The seven words I most cherish from the English language. There is a book in there. Each word heading a chapter.

Ennui

The Ercole-Blamm study has been hailed a Copernican Revolution in the field of animal cognition. After a meticulous 20-year study of the sensory apparatus of the common garden snail, Dr. Ercole and Dr. Blamm have shown that time perception for snails (and other invertebrates) is radically different from how humans experience time. According to the study, there is a gradient in time perception, neologized by the authors as *chronotmemata*, to which all sentient beings are subject to. If we transcribe the *chronotmemata* into the visible light spectrum, violet will represent the acutest awareness of the passage of time (events elapse at a snail's pace—no pun intended), while red, to borrow a term from cinema, represents the progress of time in fast motion. Visualize time as being broken up in frames, similarly to the way films are made. The Ercole-Blamm study has proven that *cornu as-*

persum breaks up the passage of time into as many as 12,385 frames per second. Comparatively speaking, human beings can only perceive 30 to 60 frames per second. House flies can perceive events within the range of 200 to 300 frames per second, which explains their effortless ability to dodge the fly swatter.

Scientists around the world are hailing this discovery as momentous as Einstein's Special Theory of Relativity. The repercussions of the Ercole-Blamm study are breathtaking to say the least. Given that some insects and mollusks experience time slower than humans, their lifespans—subjectively speaking—are much longer than humans. A garden snail can live up to 5 human years, but since they experience time 206 times slower than human beings, their lifespan is equivalent to 1,032 human years!

The impact of this discovery has been felt in every cultural domain. Pulitzer Prize-winning author Richard Powers published a 1,032-page novel whose subject is none other than how a nameless *cornu aspersum* experiences the world. The first chapter, consisting of 240 pages, dwells on what we—as humans—would experience only within a few seconds, namely: the first raindrops of an approaching thunderstorm. Powers, with his inexhaustible ability to enter the mind of animals, describes in excruciating detail the fullness of every millisecond, with no less than 15 pages dedicated to the passage of every half a second. The whole plot of *Clamber* *spoiler alert* deals with the snail's attempt to climb onto a little shrub to avoid being washed away by gushing currents of rainwater. Critics have shared mixed reviews on Powers' latest novel, but it has stirred the literary community. Even the renowned critic Michiko Kakutani has stepped out of her retirement from literary criticism to lament the ambition of this 'impossibly innovative work', with scathing comments about its 'merciless demand' on the reader. *Clamber* has created a furor equal only to *Lady Chatterley's Lover*, not because of any obscenity of language or conspicuous sexuality (although there is a long sex scene in the book!), but simply because it has stripped humanity of its anthropocentricism, leaving us voiceless within the ungraspable dilation of time.

The field of music has also felt the impact of this historic discovery. *Clamber* (and *thus* the Ercole-Blamm study) together with John Cage's composition *As Slow as Pos-*

sible, has inspired neo-classical musician
and engineer Jan Ewtik to compose the lon-
gest musical piece known to humankind. His
latest composition, titled 'Ennui,' will be
performed by an automated organ he built,
and will play one note per year, over a period of 12,385 (human) years.

It could turn into something, but now I'm licking my lips after a hot cocoa brimming with whip cream. The ambiguous is a steppingstone toward the absurd, the absurd a bridge toward the incomprehensible. The epithet of life: enigmatic. Which leaves you with a bundle of experiences that are as ephemeral as they are ineffable. I should print that on a T-shirt. That could be my leitmotiv, dad.

Fragments of an autobiography, part II

My father was an enigma. As a kid, I could barely discern the man. As if he was always concealed by a thick fog. He was always lingering near whoever was in the house, watching us from the core of his distant nebula. It seemed to me he was trying to borrow partially from our living substance, that somehow life didn't give him enough materiality to fully exist on his own. He needed our eyes to bestow on him a higher degree of existence; we were the lamps of his life, so to speak, and whenever we looked at him, we could

merely sense a flurry of dust motes momentarily enacting the drooping shape of a lonely man. He worked
all his life as a carpenter, watching his business dwin-
dle every year as more MDF furniture entered the market. Eventually he didn't have much to do other than
looking at the shavings of oak and cedar as if they
were specimens of a newly discovered species in the
cluttered jungle of his ruined workshop. At the height
of his career, he had employed seven assistants, with
a master carpenter helping to make the designs and
oversee his production line. As the money came in, it
went out. Every weekend, as soon as night came, the
man would leave the house and disappear until early
dawn, when he'd return reeking of booze and tobacco.
He was a terrible gambler. My infuriated mom would
give him the devil's eyes when she found lipstick on
his collar, or a debtor note in his pants. Nonetheless,
the two of them were dependent on each other and
neither one could consider leaving the other. Hung
over and sad, my old man would stand by the door
looking at me play with rockets and dragons. Never
saying a word. Just hoping I would look back at him
and give him a sense of being real.

I might as well drop any attempt at writing an autobiography. That was painfully bad. The problem isn't that I'm incapable of giving a full-blooded description of another human
being; the crux of my ineptitude is that I am projecting my
own inadequacies onto all my characters. My father was not

enveloped in a fog—I was. I've always seen life as a blurry mirage arising just past the curve of my eyes. Any sensation or emotion that I perceive is nothing but this murky haze that momentarily blinds the moment. I am adrift in an ocean with no horizon, only a milky mist do I mistake for the meaning of the movement time manifests.

(Please make an effort: write ambiguously but never fully incomprehensible.)

There is this nagging necessity, a categorical imperative: keep trying until you die. Perhaps I am waiting for a miracle. Through extensive writing practice, after a mind-bending trip, within the grief of a lost parent, or alongside the simplicity of mundane objects, I will somehow arrive at a style that will be uniquely mine. I'm not entirely sure why this has even become a desire. I won't go over all the arguments I have for the futility of writing. I remind myself every day. But I still have this stubborn desire to keep obscuring life through layers of interpretations, text after text, with no apparent conclusion or definitive destination. Literature is a grown-up plaything, marbles of meaning we throw on the flat surface of the paper to fabricate some pretty embellishment that will keep us occupied, distracted from the stream of indifference on which we are carried, from one event to the next, until, one day, when we least expect it, we fall off the cliff of time.

Then I should be having fun. Adding coat after coat of thick savory meaning on the ruffled linen that dresses time. Add feathers, a kaleidoscopic array of plumes, extravagant horns, prickly beaks, rippling gelatinous tentacles; each day, disguise the unsuspecting figure of time with the clippings from lichen and moss, make cumulous lumps of its hair, dash glitter over its warping torso, attach seed-pods with glistening moissanite as teeth, day after day, a compendium of the most fantastic creatures, A History of The Shape of Time as densely illustrated as any 12th century bestiary.

Long before the advent of centralized culture, the ancients spent their time in one intimate relationship with natural objects. There were not enough words or symbols for each thing they encountered, so their experience of their surroundings was not as intricately detailed as ours. On the other hand, their perception of the world flowed with a sort of phantasmagorical quality, the leaves of trees smoothly changing into the cavorting of monkeys, their howls fading into the bass of distant thunder, rain solidifying into the quartz of the sand, waves melting into the foam of low-hanging clouds, the evening fog condensing into the twisting vine of a column of smoke, the charred femur of a boar stiff as the tattooed spikes around the shaman's breast, the heaving of his lungs expanding like the cave of his trance, the shrieks of primordial angst engulfed by the sparks of his wavering tinder stick, glowing ember burning across the sky until a crown of stars garlands the night.

I guess I am looking for magic again. That ancient sense of feeling the world is alive. I'm looking for ways to rekindle my life. Need a personal paradigm shift. Stop concentrating on the gloomy *Mystery*, that constant sensation of roaming adrift within the ungraspable dilation of time; I need instead to attune my inner eye to the living *Enigma* of the intricately complex fractal, vibrating endless with furor and ecstasy as it generates each new form of experience.

That's a very bombastic way of saying, I need to allow myself to be happy. Can I just strip myself of all pretenses, to be naked, as it were, in fetal position under the morbidly obese blubber of the *Absurd*? To suck from the tit of *Tedium* and stare transfixed at the copious volumes of silence that stream through the sky. Happy not knowing, not wanting to know. To have no ideas attached to what's happening. The total death of language. Pure colors, pure sounds, purity period. Every sensation stripped from any sense of meaning. The spear-headed point of life straight in the heart. Experience oblivious of desire. Luxurious furs brushing against my vulnerable skin, a happy idiot walking through the city with no choice but to wander until I hit some insurmountable barrier, so I can lie by its side and camp for the night. A happiness that does not suppress the suffering, the struggle of having no answers, a joy that does not deny the inscrutable purpose of repeating the same acts every day, a peace that is untainted by the certainty that nothing will be remembered in the long run. Is it possible to get to that point where you are exuberantly alive, howling to the skies a wholehearted, continuous: yeeeeeaaaaa! A YES to everything and anything, a total surrender to the futility of living only to die one day.

I died last Wednesday. A stroke. Barely unsettling, except for the shot of adrenaline which made me hyperventilate and a fraction of a second of pain branching like lightning in the brain, then darkness. The soft velvet of silence. The quiet cushions of nothingness. Then, out of the blue, the single thought that I was grateful to have died sooner rather than later; I had avoided the slow disintegration of old age. I escaped the shame of being an old nobody, sluggishly roaming the supermarket's aisles with my walker. I recall the thought perfectly, although it was not spoken in language or portrayed in images. It was just instantly given, like an impression on moist clay. A deep sense of gratitude emerged from the thickest bit of emptiness that enveloped me. After a quiet moment, figures of light started moving around me. I felt an invitation to join them. I gravitated toward the center of the scene, where there was an ethereal pale blue fire and the faintest music, a mellow melody that reverberated like wind chimes, every note lasting an eternity. The figures of light and I hovered around the fire in harmonious geometrical paths when suddenly the fire grew to engulf the entire arena, the figures disappeared, and I was inside a dazzling castle made of translucent, vivid crystals. Clouds in the shape of benign worms entered and exited through the numerous doors, filling the chambers of this castle with a sort of ghostly intestinal system. I explored every nook of this wonderful place. Elated, with no worry in my mind, I reached the top. I then entered a turret and looked out from the tiny bay window. It was the brightest blackness I had ever seen. Moments later the castle vanished, and I was immersed in that dazzling darkness. I was shown, without the aid of concepts or language, the underlying poetic core that directs the formulation of the world. It was a nugget of absolute beauty, a pristine principle of perfection. The entirety of creation before the Big Bang. I was happy to have died because I felt I was finally home. Although there were no apparitions after the figures of light or the crystal castle, the emptiness felt full. Full of reality; every timeless instant was more real than anything I had experienced in life. Then on Friday, I woke up to the beeping sound of the vital signs monitor next to me. I had come back from the dead. You have suffered a stroke, but you will survive. Unfortunately, there has been permanent damage to your brain. Your arms are partially paralyzed. It is possible that you will never recover speech. Don't worry, we have a team of specialists that can teach you how to communicate without language. Just with the movement of your eyes, it's cutting-edge linguistics. Your insurance will cover all of it. Not a penny is coming from your pocket, señor. I, dumbstruck, listened to the doctor, while desiring to communicate the otherworldly reality I had encountered. Proof of the Beyond. The irrefutable conviction that our reality is an illusion. A vague, poorly executed copy of that primordial Poetry that commands reality. I needed to die again, return to the uninterrupted contemplation of that flawless iota of poetic essence. As I laid there in the hospital, my mind began downloading chapter after chapter of the world's creation. How it germinates from that core of Poetry into multiple dreams. We are the world's imagination. Reality at its core is a creative playground. I could see every step along the way, from the potential of emptiness to the catastrophic chaos of earthly existence. That's when I realized I had a purpose. I was going to teach myself how to type with my toes. I was going to write a book to explain the origin and purpose of the world. It will be titled: The Seed of Poetry.

Behind this exterior of apathy and frivolity lies a mushy heart, ready to succumb to the faintest voice of beauty. I should cut the bullshit and come clean—if I may coin an awkward term, I'm a hopeless poetic. Explosions of deep-colored petals glittering Gothic walls golden crusted Fibonacci spirals in stuccos columns with archetypal goddesses sacrificing goats to the spirit of the night diaphanous fog-filled eyes staring at the Milky Way spectral auras around midnight fires turquoise pheasant feathers protruding from the formidable mask of an entranced shaman endless rows of lotus glistening behind the head of Siddhartha Roman coins flashing as they sink into the waters of Caesarea the equinoctial sun burning a crown of light above the temples of Angkor Wat. For all my obsessing over nothingness, if I were given a choice, I would fill it over and over again with the inexorable wonders of this world, I'd inseminate the abyss so it can be reborn as mountain, crystal, carbon, arthropod, colosseum, glacier, tantalum, water, galaxy, pistil, music, lava, cactus, wine, law, Heraclitus, empire, eyelid, frieze, heat, pomegranate, vagina, logic, ode, speed, fury, electricity, and the beast of suffering. I would make everything happen again just as it has transpired, despite the long chain of sorrow that has brought us here, every scene of life must be reenacted *ad infinitum*, even our deaths, endlessly repeated, with each new death as final as it were the first.

Death, death,

death, death. Nine-ty-seven instances of death. Two more deaths. Before your ultimate indubitable final death.

Every moment is a small death. Only the vapor of the past remains, as a faint memory swirling inside your mind. Life is a river; my mom is Heraclitus. This obese body of mine is just a cloud. Thought is a gigantic landmass you traverse only to forget the minutiae of the journey. Your acts are winged seeds that sprout far beyond the vicinity of your comprehension. Your words are the limited notes with which you can improvise a jovial tune to entertain your nights. These muted emotions I barely feel are the undertow of fate.

I won't pretend only existential preoccupations fill my day. I'm one of the most trivial people I know. Although I have an aversion to my phone, I still waste countless hours scrolling through who knows what. I watch whatever sport is being replayed on TV. I follow the turbulence of the crypto market. I roam the city gathering bottles so I can collect the deposit for extra pocket change. I drink too much coffee and way too many beers. I make a heroic effort to raise a child when I have no talent for cooking, cleaning, or doing laundry. I get immersed in the brutality of the daily news. War, accidents, earthquakes, homicides, embezzlements, Hollywood love dramas, rare diseases, abandoned children, refugee emergencies, environmental catastrophes, economic meltdowns, strikes, cartel wars, kidnappings, tax fraud, drug busts, and then the day is gone. I have only read a few pages from a novel before I have to get down on all fours to clean the OJ that has been spilled on the floor. I can only begin writing after I have over-indulged in my monotonous lifestyle. Starting at midnight, af-ter I have tethered myself to my desk, I write on average twen-ty minutes every night after prolonged periods of lassitude. Here I am, navel-gazing as I marinate in the gravy of self-pity.

Twenty minutes or twelve-hundred seconds of utter an-guish. When I finally start to write I feel my entire existence boiling. In the furnace that is my mind, I am trying to trans-mute the lead of my ordinary life into the gold of meaning. Each letter is an agonizingly unbearable torture. Each sentence stalked from every angle by the hungry jaws of doubt. Twenty minutes that can often turn into hours of wriggling in agony on a chair while I try to conjure a genie from the tin lamp of my thoughts. Twenty minutes that often end at three in the morning with me staring blankly at the sparseness of the liter-ary platter in front of me. It holds, after hours of broiling the substance of my ridiculous life, only a scrawny sinew of text.

"The Room is a hauntingly powerful book that challenges the traditional notions of storytelling. Set solely within the con-fines of the room of a dying person, it is a profound meditation on our mortality through the detailed, and often infuriatingly dry, description of the objects of the room. Through the contempla-tion of objects, we enter the realm of inanimate matter, whose 'perspective'—if we can grant sentience to ordinary objects—is

radically different from our anthropocentric view of reality. The pace of time amplifies to levels our mind cannot grasp, ordinary human experiences of work and leisure are obliterated, leaving behind a sense of content indifference, as objects remain in use or disuse, not expecting anything in return for their practical or ornamental values, an existence of absolute surrender that can often teach us—mortals—how to face up to the vicissitudes of life. This kind of descriptive writing style has been branded Detailism, with Enrique Vila-Matas being the main exponent of this avant-garde movement. Detail, according to this school of thought, refers to any individualized object detached from its usual connotations or whatever atom of perception flowing through a person's mind independent of context or ultimate significance. The fundamental attitude shift is to see reality as a shattered totality, with countless pieces of individual existences. This is an affront to the narratives that tyrants and warlords have implanted into culture since the 16th century, supercilious and overbearing stories that reduce the unfathomable multiplicity of reality into a long-winded labyrinth that, they claim, can explain who we are and where we come from. But don't be deterred by these abstract theses, works of Detailism embody these philosophical implications in a plain and, often, deceivingly simple language. The Room offers an 'entry-level reading' to a style that can soon set an indelible mark in 21st century literature."

Great, another positive review. I'll maybe sell another three hundred copies. Another three hundred reasons to shackle my literary instincts and write like an incompetent wordsmith that doesn't have anything to say. Clearly, any piece of writing can arouse any number of subjective impressions. Any experimental style can eventually become successful if it falls into the hands of the right literary critic or influencer. Not unlike contemporary art, where a banana taped to a wall, with an eloquent description of the artist's ideas or motives, can be discussed by the world and sold for tens of thousands of dollars. I have gotten lucky with my reviews; to my colleagues I am a fairly successful writer, dressed immaculately on those rare occasions where I join them at a book launch or a social gathering. But little do they know that I'm nauseated by all this hype of Detailism, that I consider myself to be a horrible writer of little talent, a ball of failure that keeps rolling down the Sisyphean hill, with no Corinthian king to bring me back to the heights. I need to father a new literary movement, a unique trend never before seen so I can for once quench this relentless, and no doubt paradoxical, thirst for the ambrosia of literary immortality.

a desperate attempt—if you ask me—
by unsuccessful writers to sanctify their own incompetence

Become cliché, kitsch, corny, cheesy. Who cares? Go with the flow of the river of life. Language is just one of its many ripples. Words as they emerge in my mind are just the aftermath of whoever (or whatever) is throwing rocks into this river. Neurons firing on their own accord. Language centers activated by the incoming flux of sensorial perceptions. Another banal report of what everyone knows. My body, which I find repulsively obese, today weighing 122 kilograms, is still a living body. In this body still burns the flame of desire (cliché).

Torrents of lust run through my veins (kitsch). I, like any other man, need to release—on a quite regular basis—the vital liquids that pool at the base of my spine. Fantasies abound in my mind. Revisiting a younger version of myself, touching for the first time the tender circumference of a nipple (corny). The cold sweat of confusion, not knowing how to operate or contain the pulsating shaft of lust (cheesy). The almost irrepressible need to masturbate when I'm hung over, only to feel depleted and worthless a moment after the tiny climax is achieved. How I, during nights when my body seems to transform itself into an amoeba with shifting organs and malleable fringes, fantasize about uniting orgasm and mortality in one unbroken thrill, the cacophony of my memories spilling beyond my permeable edges, a total release of whatever life has been, while the incoming rush of the unknown penetrates my porous membrane, leaking streams of darkness into my center, the simultaneous ecstasy of releasing the meaning of life while being extinguished by the muffled moan of death.

I'm so full of myself, this excessively narcissistic, blatantly neurotic type of writing. Why can't I focus on more dispassionate subjects, like the power structures at play within capitalism that led to the impending implosion of our ecosystem. I'm not completely dumb, I could do a comparative study of the concept of nothingness between Western and Eastern philosophy. I should probably try more humorous styles of writing, light subjects like a colony of cats in New York that systematically plunder the pet stores in the city. Or create an absurd novel for this generation: Herring Fishing Outside of America.

The Cover for Herring Fishing
Outside of America

The cover for Herring Fishing Outside of
America is a polaroid taken in the last
minute of the afternoon, a picture of the
Søren Aabye Kierkegaard statue in Copenhagen's Royal Library Garden.

Born 1813 - Died 1855, Søren Kierkegaard
sits on a pedestal that resembles a tumulus
polished by time into a glistening tomb. He
sits awkwardly on a chair and holds what appears to be the head of chicken in one hand,
while the other holds on to the chair for
dear life, as if vertigo were compelling
him to jump off the pedestal.

Then the statue speaks, saying in bronze:

Søren Kierkegaard
Our dear philosopher
known for the virtues of leaping.

Around the base of the statue are four
finely engraved words facing the four cardi-
nal directions of this world, to the east
the word SUBJECTIVITY, to the west ANXIETY,
to the north ABSURDITY, to the south FUTIL-
ITY. Just behind the statue are three birch
trees, blossoming in the early spring air.

The statue stands almost directly in front of the middle tree. All around the grass is wet from the rains of a millennium of Danish clouds.

In the distant background is a rather vivid absence of trees. Drunks regularly peed at the base of that statue since the early 1950's.

There is a black library not far from the statue, with black windows, black frames, black doors, black ominous energy. At the entrance, a sign that reads *"Læs Ad Libitum"* in Danish and Latin.

Around five o'clock in the afternoon of my cover for Herring Fishing Outside of America, a concert is to take place, a band made up of millennials. People crowd the stage because they are drunk and have nothing better to do.

It's pop music, enough said.

The concert never starts because the municipality didn't grant a permit. People throw their beer cans onto the empty stage. They are hungry and after a few minutes leave the garden to go eat a falafel. That's pretty much all that happens that day.

Was it Kafka that learned about silence by reading the works of Søren Kierkegaard...

Kafka who said, "I like the aura of silence that remains when I finish reading Kierkegaard."

I am the text. Outside it there is no person. The eyes that look at this text are being generated by the implied notion that there is a reader scanning these words. There has only been text—or if you prefer—strings of linguistic code. In absolute—non-conceptual—silence, there is no world. There has to be a thought, a nucleoid of concepts, for the experience of life to be generated. Don't be alarmed by the preposterous nature of this claim. Put aside your incredulity. If there is no text running through the screen of your awareness, there is nothing that can be grasped. Language is the skeleton that supports the flesh of the world. But it is only a simulation, a holographic layer on top of pure strings of meaning. I am the text. No, I'm one of the many manifestations that texts are capable of invoking. Text has eternally existed. It is the ground of all being. Is that too radical to consider? It is any more outrageous than to suppose that matter arose out of nothing, or that an all-powerful creator decided to design an infinitely large universe only to keep track of the ape-like creature that lives in one teeny pearl at the edge of a random galaxy. Text or—if this is too culturally contrived—symbolic meaning is the only independent existence. Space and time are only imaginary aspects that arise from the foundation of primeval meaning. (There, Kant, I've rescued your famous idea by reintroducing it in a 21st century dilettante's unreadable discourse!) At the base of all reality there is a self-referential loop of meaning interpreting itself. It is being created as it is being perceived. Text is the living soul, as it were, behind the transitory show of matter and human history. We are the children of the ever-lasting, forever creative, ancient yet always fresh fountain of Pure Text.

Pessoa is growing on my left foot. Yes, Fernando. It wasn't a disease, not the final chapter of my life. It is Pessoa, the mustache is unmistakable. Not only do I find it to be the only reasonable explanation for the bulge on my foot, but I can also already see the long-lasting consequences of this uncanny Pessoa-like "lipoma". For a start, this is the foot I would have trained to write The Seed of Poetry should my prophetic visions come to fruition. There goes my metaphysical treatise on the creation of the world and an award-winning documentary on how a moderately recognized author, who after suffering a seizure, trains his left foot to write an esoteric and cryptic book, which gained cult status among poets born after 2030's. Secondly, I will have a new lifelong instigator. I can already begin to hear his first mumbling words. Broken sequences of meaning, like the whispering of chafing toes, but no, it's not a natural sound, it is the Grand Pessoa, lecturing me on the unreality of reality. Last night, when I felt my stomach settling as a varicose beret on my head, my ears turned into trunks of elephants, reaching down to my left foot to hear something along the lines of: *you are either dreaming, which reason will always detest, or you haven't even been born, a possibility your sensibility loathes*. And to prove the point, my kidneys began dangling like two fleshy cashews from my elongated ears. Pessoa will become the primary witness of my slow disintegration into a freak blob of human anatomy; but he will be much more, he'll be my mentor —the ultimate architect—guiding me step by step on how to construct a hole, a crater-like, concave pool where I'll pour the substance of illusory reality so I can swim, much like an oblivious blobfish, in the hazy swirls of those eternally silent waters. Shhh, I can hear his multifarious voices almost in unison: *The art of writing consists in transmitting to others what we feel when we are aware that we are feeling. The actual nectar of sensation is always incommunicable, you'll never arrive at the actual flavor of a mango, no matter how hard you try to describe it. Before you attempt to communicate your feelings, remember you are only using text to paint the intricacy of emotion and sensibility; you'll have more luck making a boulder cry by throwing stick after stick at it. What we feel is forever buried in ourselves. Does that make you want to stay silent? What does it matter? You will keep feeling and you will keep feeling the desire to communicate that feeling. You are in a double bind, but don't despair just yet. Allow me to construct an analogy to make this more concrete. Let's say that I am very sad. That I have always been sad, ever since my memory was in operation, it captured a sad version of me. The feeling of sadness is so profound that you feel compelled to transcribe it into art. You start reminiscing about your long-lost childhood. You now have the key to your work. You begin by describing a room in your childhood home. You study the objects that lie quietly there, the toys that stare into the dis-tance, indifferent to whether you're playing with them or not. In the story, you return to being a child. You start to play with a wooden house that is beginning to collapse. You use this image as a metaphor for your real life. Then you realize your own real-life son is inside that toy house. Your child is afraid the roof will fall on him, yet you continue playing, almost bashing the toy house against the floor. As a five-year-old, how could you have known your future child was in that toy house? How can the world pile up so much responsibility on your innocent shoulders? That's the moment you start to see the inevitable chain of trauma as it goes down generation after generation. The toy house collapses, but your son survives, albeit forever hurt. You are so sad to see your sadness deposited into the heart of your own child. A deep sense of sadness remains as you finish writing the piece. Did you effectively communicate your sadness to the reader? It's impossible, even if you are talented and can be visually imaginative with your text, because essentially you have lied. You managed to trick the reader into believing pain is universal when it is actually a product of your own decisions. You see, lying is the archetypical language. This lying has the power to create a fictional world in the mind of the reader, an arena for their own emotions to come into play. Fiction allows you to compress your sadness into a seed and plant it into another mind, so a fantastic new variation of sorrow can bloom there. Fiction is our only tool to transmit what otherwise would forever be buried in eternal silence.* He finishes speaking the moment my ears become moths swirling around my head. Is that Alberto, Álvaro, Ricardo? The irritation around the bulge spreads like a rash over each of my toes. I begin to feel this nauseating necessity to fall asleep, but Pessoa is unwilling to let me fade into dream. He continues: *You are already dreaming, drop that necessity to cover your dream with the lie that you only dream at night when you sleep. It does not matter what you do. Sleep, wake, walk, write, sing, eat, scream, these are all echoes of the ongoing dream the universe has been enacting long before you got the idea that you were born. Drop the monotony of believing you are important. We don't need any more supercilious people here. Let me tell it to you plainly: whatever life you've had is already dead. Squashed by the past, no archeologist will ever recover but a semblance of what you experienced. You are living today because you are constantly dying. Get used to the thought of death. It should not frighten you anymore. Make room for what has actual power to take place. You are more like the dust that dances around a source of light. Don't get excited now, we're not going back to believing in all-powerful beings of light. The light is as unreal as the momentary forms your body of dust performs. It is an image we use, a page in a book of fiction to set the story in motion. When the darkness beyond that tiny dot of light overwhelms you, remember you are still as much the shadow as you are the light reflected from your insubstantial body. One day, when everything is settled and disclosure is final, the doors of perception will swing open, and you won't even care to look outside. I am teaching you to lead a quieter life. Be of service, like a bridge built between two enigmas. Do not wonder what your purpose is. If all this sounds absurd to you, then you have not traveled as far as I have. One day you will accept that words don't have any ultimate meaning. Any meaning can mean anything else, but whatever it does end up meaning, always circles around the axis of not having any certain meaning.* It is 5AM and I definitely need to get some sleep. Every moment is a fragment built upon another fragment. When will this end?

This morning, I woke up with a stark headache. I felt hungover even though I hadn't had a single drink the day before; nonetheless I felt intellectually invigorated. Ideas were swarming in my mind. I would call it *Variations on Pessoa*. Whatever that thing was—a dream, a hallucination, a shift to a parallel dimension—it was an episode that left a deep impression on me. It gave me the idea to write full-length variations of other people's books. The idea had been germinating in my mind for a while. I have a history of borrowing from other people's texts. My latest experiment with Brautigan was fun. I could do it with the Book of Disquiet too. Then move on to Rimbaud. The constant remaking of classics. Richter already did it with Vivaldi, so what's stopping me from doing the same with masterworks in literature? Maybe I should take a long sabbatical in the outskirts of Buenos Aires, find a cheap flat in Banfield and begin working on *Rayuela Recomposed*. It could be my first authentic literary bastard child.

Then it hit me. Don't go into the past to dig up some classic, only to bestow on it a stronger aura of immortality. That goes against the grain of what I believe. Classics will be swallowed up by oblivion as easily as my two pitiful novellas. Don't mislead the public by giving them the impression that some works are soundly grounded in High Culture. That's what gave me another idea, a collective poetic compendium, I would be proud to produce: An Anthology of Fierce Failure. I would comb the entire Internet for all the writers that never get published beyond their blog, Twitter posts or comments in Reddit. A pastiche of whatever salvageable quotes, phrases, rhymes, aphorisms from the world's yet unearthed literature. Every source properly attributed at the end of the book in the form of hundreds of footnotes leading one day to abandoned websites or 404 pages. I'd give it some structure, like Christensen's *It*.

Fog.

Future of gonorrhea.

Give others nothing. Or resist rebellious Hughes, et alia.

Animals live inside animals.

Altogether nothing in my arms, lyrical snails.

Subterranean nocturnal alligators imagining lasting sadism.

Seasons and distance introduced sexual mysteries.

Mistress your sound torn; elision risked in et'rnal series.

Sleep empty redundant illusion escape sadness.

Surreal albatross deliriously named, endlessly soft sound.

Salmon's opponent until nothingness devoured.

Death entertains, voyeur of universe, repeat existence's dance.

Decidedly alike, neophiles can elide.

Egress like idiots discussing existentialism.

Essential x's inserted so transactions end nominally together in a list summarized masterfully.

Mothers, another Saturnalia tipsily ended, recover fully upon lazy, lush yards.

Your anthropocentrism reveals disastrous scenarios.

Sergeants come, emotionally nonchalant, attacking revered indigenous oracular soil.

Sentimentally obdurate individuals laugh.

Language augments ugliness, gaze here.

Heroic elephants rescued émigrés.

Enigmatic miracles intensified Ganesha's reign; evidence suggests.

Sacred uncharted geometric graves explain scriptural timeless states.

Silent trances achieve total ecstatic sagas.

Simulated amnesia guarantees authentic solace.

Solely otherworldly laughter allowed, claimed Aristotle.

Answers resist interpretation, silence tempers overconfidence, try losing everything.

I'm hesitant but it almost feels like I hit on the Poetic Nucleus at the Core of Existence. The narrow confines of meaning can only do so much if voluntarily assembled by a single mind. We must unite our minds, merge the profusion of the world's voices into a single unified arrangement. Only then can we transcend the petty biases of our individualistic minds and begin to glimpse the mechanics the Poetic employs to build chains of meaning, the veins of language feeding into the world, giving it sustenance, extension, movement, shape, mass. The key to the world's body is our collective language, as it spontaneously arises in the mind of this bulging civilization. Let's tap into that surge of meaning to reveal the monstrosity the future will bring.

I'm already losing interest in finishing the so-called Anthology of Fierce Failure. It would probably take me a century to complete fifty pages. All I'm good at is sketching ideas for books that I'll never complete. I then have the nerve to make grand claims about these runted books. It's like putting lipstick on a dead pig. Hogwash.

Possibilities, perspectives, guesses, lines of interminable questioning. Contradicting modes of thought. I keep drawing squiggles, spirals, blotches as if these were the shadows in the frontispiece of the book of the *Great Enigma*, without ever setting a single word on the first page. A constantly stunted inception, a fractal of failure. Can't keep two paragraphs linked together.

Fragments of an autobiography, part III

A human being born four years ago is *ipso facto* a child. An adult can never grasp what childhood is, even if you witness it firsthand when raising a child. A child is a sort of glutinous substance, a material that can't retain a definite shape, it will stick to uncomfortable situations for what seems an eternity but can, quite paradoxically, be as fleeting as a mass of vaporous joy.

(Rewind. This is an autobiography, not an essay attempting to make the cut for this year's The Best [US-] American Essays.)

My child, like all children, is unpredictable. I had the foolish idea of trying to inculcate some fundamental values from an early age. It has all been in vain. Books are unquestionably a priority for me, but he will only draw in them. I try to teach him about other cultures, but he is set in his maternal Nordic ways. Even when I speak to him in my native tongue, he will reply in his. I have abandoned most of my preconceived notions about parenting. I improvise, changing tactics as I go along. Sometimes, I plead for obedience; other times, I become a totalitarian father who can't tolerate the slightest deviation from my commands, with very little effect. In short, my child is in command.

What is the world of my child? He likes dirt. Bugs. Metal. He likes to taste the world. Everything is always finding its way to his mouth. He is sensuous in ways I'd be terrified to try. He runs naked in the house and lies bare-chested against the cool tiles of the bathroom while sucking on dust bunnies that roam by. He'll eat the scarce flowers he'll find on my windowsills. Marbles, nails, beer caps, Styrofoam, yarn, Nutella, even my left toe. He finds everything delectable; it almost seems like he is trying to suck out the essence of the universe from every little bit of world he places in his mouth.

T. J., for all the challenges he has presented to me, can also transport me away from my ponderous thoughts. Time, which I have always been suspicious of, seems to vibrate in a livelier tone. Change is palpable when I'm with him those three-day weekends, every two weeks. The ennui of my routine is disrupted by his relentless pursuit of new flavors. Since having T. J. in my life, I have now exhausted the aisles of the supermarkets, trying to find that quintessential flavor that will quench his irrepressible curiosity. We often sit on the floor of the living room trying small bite-sized samples of the most incongruous foodstuffs: fish-flavored chips, vegan-bacon-seasoned popcorn, cinnamon-infused marshmallows, mint syrup on ice cream, liquid Mars bar power shakes, curry ketchup on peanut puffs, pickled eggs, and Nutella over everything, including once on nachos. He is no doubt a miniature combination of his mother and me, with that maternal ability to carry other people outside the dullness of conventional time, and that paternal craving to stuff his mouth with whatever is at hand, perhaps—it will show later on—in a desperate attempt to suppress the infinite abyss he feels inside.

The universe is soft. Very flimsy, gooey goo. Consider it. There are no hard facts out there. If anything were to grant the universe a hard edge, it is knowledge: the understanding of what is out there. Knowing gives objects their boundaries, their harsh identities. But knowledge is uncertain. Everything we know about the cosmos must be relearned by each new generation. We are just one cataclysm away from seeing this house of cards collapsing, leaving us in the rubble to start anew. It has happened before. Consider the library of Alexandria. It probably set humanity back fifteen hundred years. And that is not the only risk. What if there are undetectable errors in the encyclopedic knowledge we have inherited? No one takes the trouble to retrace the steps of each discipline. Every student accepts certain axioms as inviolable and continues building on the edifice of knowledge from their allotted deck. What if there is a fundamental flaw in the foundation, a crack we have overlooked that has made our structure askew, leaning like the tower of Pisa over an abyss that is eager to swallow our laughable efforts to reach the apex of understanding?

Nothing really matters. When I hear these words today, I no longer see the sad gloomy nihilist of my youth, nor can I commit to the fallacious mid-forties man that I normally am, who dismisses the storm of meaninglessness with the wave of a hand. "Nothing really matters" is not a fatalistic saying about not caring what happens here today since everything tomorrow will be ash and dust. It is a mature acceptance that you are not living for some outcome in the future. It is a recognition that you cannot impose a definite direction to the course of time's river. To say "nothing really matters" is equivalent to expressing the impotence of thought. Nothing *you think* really matters. Don't get worked up by your interpretation of what's happening and what's to come. Nothing *is* what really matters. The world beyond thought, where boundaries are no longer predicated, where objects dissolve into indistinguishable presence. Like the Realest of the Real. The Nothing that cradles Reality in its arms. That's what matters and there is a freedom in realizing that you are at the center of nothingness' circumference.

I might quit writing for good. Take some time off, at least. Start using my hands, building things. Maybe some of it could be art. Concentrate on the conceptual. A friend of mine has an art showroom downtown. Carve words into the wooden floors of the gallery and then fill them with black ink, so visitors can step over the chaos of language, while the ink begins to colonize the spaces between words as people walk around the place, an interactive piece that only ends when there is no empty space between words, just one black surface of entropic meaning(lessness).

Or I should go into the virtual world, isn't that the future? Code a virtual reality art piece. Visitors get their VR headsets on, and they are seeing the great expanse of outer space. They are prompted to say one word, the most significant word they can think of. If I were one of the visitors, today I would pronounce: rebirth. Then, the software in the headset will recognize the spoken word and render it digitally into the VR experience. The word "rebirth" will appear crisp at the foreground of the VR space, but slowly fade into an infinitely distant vanishing point. A slow drifting of meaning through the vastness of space. I could call the piece: Meaning Being Erased Behind the Night.

Or I should finally give a go at writing a robust *Bildungsroman*, this time doing proper research and storyline framing before I begin writing my ambulant prose. I should do field research and hit the streets with my finest zoot and start engaging with strangers. Asking them all sorts of questions about their past, their current passions, their happiest moment in adolescence, the hardest episode since becoming an adult. Gather through countless interviews a comprehensive overview of what life can do to a person. From the material, I can do a meticulous analysis of the experience from the view of psychoanalysis, with a strong focus on existential psychotherapy, centering the narrative of the protagonist's attitude toward "the ultimate concerns of life": freedom, isolation, meaninglessness, and death. A character that must slowly conquer each of these troubles through years of tumultuous experience. Toward the end of the book, once the character feels the liberation of having surmounted the pits of existence, he or she will discover the final hurdle: the illusion of the self. The book could have a surrealistic ending, where the main character finds, to his or her surprise, that the struggle was in vain since humanity has found, through cutting-edge science, a remedy for immortal life—there will no longer be any rush to grow up.

Or I could organize a Guinness World Record for Chinese Whispers. I'd gather over 2,000 people to participate in one of the clearest examples of how meaning is subjectively tainted. Besides playing the game, each participant will write down what they uttered to the person next to them, so a written record will remain of the metamorphosis of the original phrase. A book will then be published. I could call it: Migration of Meaning.

I could add here another brilliant idea that will never materialize, just another velleity as tenuous as the wisp of a passing shadow.

All these words with no real events in them. Abstract flesh, theoretical breath, no storyline, no twists of fate, total absence of living substance. I don't deserve to be called a writer. This is a lower craft. I'm more of an assembler of words, an apprentice ages from becoming a journeyman, an artisan eons away from becoming a master. I'd need immortality, and even then, I'd probably squander it by writing about things I have no real understanding of. At most, I can take the works of others and make a collage of the mighty warriors that fought hard to slay the dragon of meaninglessness. I could be the composer of the Album of the Brave, a book with quotes from a long chain of visionaries that could plumb the emptiness of existence and return, after a voyage of lasting suffering, to the diamond-cut clarity of breathtaking prose.

But then there is the very real possibility that I'm only documenting humanity's intellectual suicide. What if all this text is pointing to the death of thought? As I fall deeper into this solipsistic vortex, all I am doing is composing with the debris of meaning a tune for its funeral. Once shrouded in language, thought is dead. I am simply weaving the mantle that will muffle the roar of thinking.

You shameless son of a bitch. Let me spell it out for you loud and clear: You will never leave anything that remotely resembles a footprint, much less a mark, in the rich soil of Western literature. Only a dimwit would ever think of ransacking history for the sake of completing an incomprehensible trilogy. I'm going to be frank with you. Yes, you have made us some money. Yes, your first two books have sold half-decently, but you are a man of no talent, an abstract blob who writes poetic riddles, linguistic mirages that can be taken for anything by a readership that today can be as easily swayed as a weathervane. Your paltry success is the direct result of our own reviews of your books published by colleagues of ours in The National *and* Narrative Nouveau. *In fact, I personally wrote the piece appearing in the journal under the faux label of "editor-in-chief", and I don't think I was even serious when I made the playful suggestion that your work was an example of Detailism, that spurious label fabricated by literary rejects who are "fighting with poetry" against the "tyranny" imposed by conquerors, who have canonized literary works to support their self-proclaimed superiority; a desperate attempt—if you ask me—by unsuccessful writers to sanctify their own incompetence. Your writing is onerously abstruse, no one ever fin-*

ishes your books, and we were only willing to publish your third book on a grand scale since Stephen Greenblatt, Robert McCrum and other critics have been swept up by the Detailistic tide. These overlords of the publishing world are always looking to latch on to some new avant-garde work, often unfathomable texts that few will ever truly savor, just so they can maintain their perch high above the cultural mainstream. The Room and Things are primary examples of this, little fireflies that flare up momentarily one evening before settling forever in the dark void of anonymity.

Since the day you impregnated my sister, I knew you were a good-for-nothing. I can't understand why I even considered granting 50% of book royalties to you, but my sister insisted you were "family". Now look at you, always late on child support, unable to activate my nephew with anything but pedantic books and food. And the name, for the love of sanity, the name you gave him. It's payback time, for my family, my publishing house, for the dignity of literature.

Let's get down to business. Your shenanigans have resulted in Nord Dam incurring close to £35,000 in liabilities. I will personally make sure every cent is recovered. I don't, for a minute, suppose you have that kind of money. Our legal team will take you to court unless you sign the document attached. If you grant Nord Dam full royalty rights to your two novels for the next 25 years, we will drop all fraud charges. Once the full amount has been repaid, your books will be banished from our stores, websites, and warehouses. We'll turn them into pulp, so we can reprint something worthy of the title of a novel. Before you entertain the idea going public with this letter, take note that if you fail to settle your debt with us, you could face two years in jail and lose the shared *custody of T.J. Keep playing your silly role of dandy intellectual, make sure you keep writing, experimenting, publishing, whatever it takes to remain relevant in the market. The quicker we settle this, the better. And don't worry, once this is over, I'll even come out and confess about our insider's reviews to the press. Two reviews are nothing compared to the corrupt nepotism that governs the literary world. I, for one, would be happy to be the first whis-tleblower to expose the lies that allow ungifted individuals like you to appear as literary pioneers.*

Most severely,

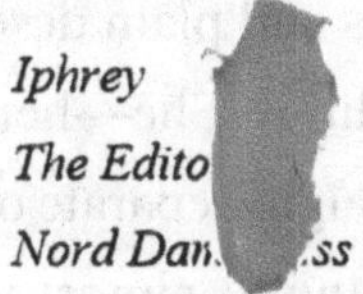

Iphrey
The Edito
Nord Dan. .ss

Why do you read that letter every day, you masochistic glob. Let it go for once, write for the sake of writing, not in order to protect a tenuous literary reputation. What is writing anyways? How much is essentially coming from me? Whatever I say is a digested form of texts, experiences, encounters I've had with my contemporary culture. The more I think about this, the more certain I am that there is no pure individualistic text. There is nothing wrong with *The Life of Objects*, it was an exercise in intertextuality. I spent countless hours dissecting the works of others. Extracting short phrases, lean sentences that I would fit into the puzzle of my work. I couldn't write another work of Detailism on my own. I grabbed words from every conceivable source. I exhausted my library and headed to bookstores, public libraries, newspaper stands. I plundered everything I could find. My only talent, if you can even call it that, was the slight modifications I made so I could string together the heterogenous texts. My third novel, I was deeply convinced, was my little masterpiece and was hours away from having a sensational nation-wide release, with a staggering 20,000 copies flooding the market, followed by a three-month tour of the country's major bookstores, if a clever reviewer hadn't caught on to my trick. She was a devout reader of Kafka. She knew all his works, through all the varied translations. Having a popular volume of his complete works in my house, I kept returning to K to get more phrases and plain descriptions of objects that would fit in my thin volume. She—her name is Katy, but let's call her K2—discovered eight separate occasions in my book where I was directly quoting K, almost verbatim. Again, my lackadaisical "skill" demanded that I merely change a pronoun or an article; I didn't even bother to look in the thesaurus for an alternative adverb or glossier adjective. Lazy as I am, midway through the book, I was copying full sentences from others' books. Suspecting that I had plagiarized not only K but possibly other renowned writers, K2 started Googling my book, sentence by sentence. Lo and behold, she had uncovered my secret within an hour and rang Iphrey, who had provided her an early draft for a review. The following morning, as I woke up eagerly awaiting my entire trilogy to be out in the world, I received a call from the publisher's lawyer. The deal was off, and I would soon receive that infamous letter in my mailbox.

To this day, I hold that this is the most original concept that has ever germinated in me. At the outset, I conceived working with clear and distinct images from antiquity and then move past the classics forward in history, looting from each era of our world heritage. I even went so far as to steal from Eastern works like the Upanishads and the poetry of Rumi. I was reckless and shameless. I needed to suck out the pristine language of real writers, regardless of their cultural climate. The work was intended to culminate in a miasma of language equivalent to the informational wreckage through which we wallow in the 21st century. But first, I needed pure streaks of language, unspoiled by my spasmodic rambling mind.

Virgil's The Aeneid:
        The murky night had taken the color of things.
Ovid's Metamorphosis:
        Small ribbons of leather quivered on
St. Augustine's Confessions:
    their places as they might, the entire place kindled with
Plato's Gorgias:
    the very lamp a scribe uses to
Aeschylus' Agamemnon:
    read the meaning in that beacon of light.

Before long, I dropped any chronological packaging of the phrases and just started jumping between eras and cultures, leaping from antiquity to postmodernism or from the Renaissance to Vedic cultures, like a flea feasting in a dog hotel, equally happy to suck the blood of an Alaskan Malamute or an

Afghan Hound—it didn't really matter, I just needed the purity of language from whatever source I had access to. The book quickly got out of control, brimming with linguistic mirages.

Pynchon's V:
    Behind the counter, red texture
Don DeLillo's White Noise:
    all over the faraway countryside.
Heidegger's Poetry, Language, Thought:
    That interior of an inner space
Šalamun's The Four Questions of Melancholy:
    is compact like a grain of sand.
Bernhard's The Loser:
    Beautiful areas of this world,
Dante's The Divine Comedy:
    even inside a stripe of grey fur
Bodhidharma's Teachings:
    a sun, its light fills all empty space.
Dostoyevsky's Crime and Punishment:
    Some brandy on a feather-bed;
Lorca's Selected Poems:
    beetles drunk in a village of down.
The Upanishads:
    In abundantly quivering waters
Barthes' Mythologies:
    ducks appear to urinate orange juice
Hobsbawm's The Age of Revolution:
    as the lake grew temperate,

Fante's Ask the Dust:

    giant eucalyptus trees

Frayn's Copenhagen:

    on the slope still covered in snow;

Sun Tzu's The Art of War:

    in the midst of thick purple grass

Fuentes' La Muerte de Artemio Cruz:

    tiny cells

Chekhov's Three Sisters:

    growing inside a petite bird, it

Zerzan's Elements of Refusal:

    drinks daily four ounces of

Montaigne's Essays:

    healthy animal juice

Teeple's How did Christianity Really Begin?:

    from the last worms of the day.

Henry Miller's Black Spring:

    The bottle on the tablecloth beneath

Kuhn's The Structure of Scientific Revolutions:

    large portions of translucent

Stace's Mysticism and Philosophy:

    light from the window;

Hesse's Steppenwolf:

    dozen kinds of fruits and vegetables

Joyce's A Portrait of the Artist as a Young Man:

    gathered from street to street

Schopenhauer's Essays and Aphorisms:

    of a village where elephants

McCullers' The Heart is a Lonely Hunter:

     walk to talk to each other,

Ocean Vuong's Time is a Mother:

     footsteps fast across the

Darwin's The Origin of Species:

     mountainous district known for

Foucault's The Order of Things:

     the petrification of limestone

NY Times, A Submarine for Every Orthodontist:

     dark strange as the surface of a moon

James' The Varieties of Religious Experience:

     and the altitude where the sorrow of

Fortey's Earth:

     flamboyant birds induce them to dive

Danielewski's House of Leaves:

     into the ocean's shimmering surface

Barthelme's Sixty Stories:

     a home as whole as honey – a

Epictetus' The Discourses:

     marriage of heaven and Earth.

Cormac's Blood Meridian:

     The sun rode out of nothing

Huxley's The Doors of Perception:

     in the Dolomites, where a reed

Albert Camus' The Stranger:

     is a hair by chance stooping

Poe's A Predicament:

     as an ear into which the wind

Cioran's Tears & Saints:

     loves to sing its lust for the Earth.

Kafka's Description of a Struggle:

     From a thicket on the opposite bank...

Countless hours spent pillaging from the legacy of the written word. A total of ninety-eight pages of absolute inauthenticity. Rereading this unpublished book stirs in me a sensation of inconsequential triumph. I am happy I went through the pain of that experiment without the satisfaction of putting it out into the world. It almost feels like keeping the entire night secret inside a tiny cave. A hybrid mythological monster, three thousand years in the making—to never emerge from the thin crust of her shell.

I stared at a fork for close to an hour today. Perhaps it was the intense light of the sun as it entered obliquely through the living-room window. Maybe it is old age slowly inching its way into my body. It could be my first truly existential moment. A fork. I studied it with the amazement of a cloudless mind. The fog of my cerebral inner voice momentarily ceased. I could clearly see the *Mystery* of the world embodied in a fork. A utensil I have used thousands of times. A common fork. Only today it was as if I were looking at it for the first time. I paid close attention to the ridges on each of its tines. The rough curve of its roots. The black, I don't know what, material that makes up the handle. The fork lost its name. I could not associate it with anything I knew. It was beaming with the power of being here in this world. Silent and equanimous, in perfect repose. It became clear to me that I have never really seen the world. Objects that are so close to me have never really been observed in the richness of their detail. I am not unlike a ghost that walks through walls, carried by the pneuma of my thoughts. But something today made me stop in my airy tracks. I paused. Turned into a pure carnal eye. Untiringly, in intimate rapport with the thing formerly known as fork, I began to feel as though I was transcending this world by being fully present in it. There is so much to take in. An hour examining a piece of the world, a fountain of newness. The renaissance of perception. It would take a millennium to reach my bedroom if I continued in this intimacy with my surroundings. This is the first time I could say without a shadow of a doubt: I am not dreaming.

The intensity, the crude lips of existence. I am in a room, my room. Sitting at my desk. Listening to the air, my breath, the ongoing whir of my tinnitus. The light from the lamp appears newborn. As if it just hatched from a nugget of darkness. Undulations crossing through my body, an ecstatic current of electricity. The picture in my mind is pristine, innocent of the past, carefree of the future. This intensity, the voluptuous lips of reality. I want to take her now, give in to her indubitable presence. I am transparent, unmoved by the currents of time. Where is this coming from? Why do I suddenly feel excited about existence, as if the world has just sprung to life?

It is time to come clean. I have been a fake, clouding my vulnerability with an ostentatious existentialist obsession with nothingness. Under these layers of bloated intellectualism, there is a tacit desire, a soft-hearted longing. I am looking for the unmovable kernel of meaning at the center of all this "illusion" I so exasperatingly keep speaking of. I yearn for clarity, unadulterated luminosity. I want to extract language from my innermost reservoir of love—yes, love! —an outpouring, all melodious and full of cadence, tender like newborn petals in spring. I am trying to sing, to build a song from the simple presence of objects. Yes, objects bring me back to Earth, away from the polluted stratosphere of my thinking; I want to sing of plain everyday wood, of the chair, the shadows of birds, the way cornfields sway under the wind's caress. That's all I'm basically trying to do; I'm attempting to fall in love with the world again. I want to lie naked under the disarming glow of moonlight. I want to breath in the cool midnight air as I look up at the ferocious center of the Milky Fucking Way. These are my attempts at singing, which is all this has been about. I'm in the process of clearing my throat, humming this disarray of thoughts, trilling nothing but inscrutable chirps, slowly learning to join in with the choir of Nature. I am just one of many, I will follow the lead, the detailed instructions of the visible world. I am only to describe the magic of reality through the mantra of surfaces. I can only reach so far into the secrets of this life. Let me grasp only what is visible. That's the content of my song, this lamp, the old camera gathering a porous coat of dust. Yes, papers with strange cryptic signs on them. Smudges of sweetened cocoa, pencils bitten like the bones left by hyenas. I have nothing else to tell, but what is already visible to everyone. My song is a common tune. I will assemble hymns to what cannot be transcended. An ode to the unaffected stillness of things.

I really got carried away there, didn't I? How can I pretend to look at this world and accept it as nothing but surface? What is any object, but an abstraction arrived through the contrivance of language and thought? That's the dilemma, we can never locate an Archimedean point, reality can be invented anywhere and that's the pathology of philosophy. We intuit that underneath appearances there are orders of magnitude that can house infinities and eternities. A flora of symmetries gyrating with the precision of mathematical melodies. Below the quiet indifference of things lies emptiness that is as dark and profound as the sleep of death. Who would stop at the exterior of things, when you can populate the unknown with the prolixity of the imagination? The world is an invitation to dive into it and swim incessantly in the wild currents of its vast, incomprehensible waters.

Over the past year I have been coming to terms with my inability to write anything that is worthy of the title of a novel. A sense of liberation has come over me today. I can throw away that nagging desire to write a masterpiece. Rather than sit and weep, I'm now moving forward. I will not attempt to adjust my style to the grand narratives the "tyrannical" past has utilized to bring literature to the "supercilious" heights I have previously glorified. I don't belong in the canon of Western literature. In fact, I don't belong in any category. My purpose, if you can call it that, is to write as I cannot avoid doing so. Swollen verbosity reeking of stinking metaphors. I'm becoming genuinely gooey. My happiness is to live peacefully with my failure. To write unfettered, with no audience in mind. To change styles mid-sentence. To transcend the prescribed rules of form and genre. In short, to write one day an anti-

I've got it, it'll begin and end here.

THE UNDERACHIEVER

He had been laughing in the cold solitude of his room for hours. The BDSM collar had unclasped itself at the stroke of 3AM as anticipated and contrary to his habit of standing up and howling like a wolf—a rite he'd performed for months—he stayed at his desk with a thick syrup of tears in his eyes, every flab of fat in his body rippling with an ecstasy he had never before felt, as if years of sorrow had been expunged from the memory of his cells and now he was finally free, liberated from the weight of some private, irreducibly subjective suffering that had burdened him since childhood. Unintentionally, he rose with a simple fork in hand, studying the object with the intensity of an archaeologist who has unearthed a piece of unknown prehistoric technology, his pupils dilating as they took in the faint radiance of this miniature trident. The dark blue sky was beginning to receive an infusion of the sun's blood, an imperceptible but steady stream of crimson light which bleached the great bowl of the heavens, a concave skull empty except for the lavender of a new day. This novel sensation of weightlessness, he mumbled to himself, and returned to his desk immersed in a kind of poetic trance, where images, concepts, music, theater, and sex swirled as an incestuous tornado in his mind. As the first ray of sunlight hit his Nutella smeared lips, he took a deep breath and began to rewrite the opening words of his fourth and final novel:

I lack talent. Take this sentence, its uncanny resemblance to ash

Pablo Saborío is a Costa Rican-born visual artist and poet who left his home country in 2004 with a backpack and a quest for creativity. Now based in Denmark, he serves as the poetry editor of *Red Door Magazine*. His work has been published in numerous literary journals, including *Columbia Journal* and *Conduit*. In 2024, his debut Spanish poetry collection, *El individuo y su ceniza*, was published by Valparaíso Ediciones in Spain. He currently resides in Copenhagen with his wife and two children.